The Education
of a Cuckold

The Education of a Cuckold

A Story of Love, Lust, and Fate

Alex Hathaway

fannypress

Seattle, WA

fannypress

Fanny Press
PO Box 70515
Seattle, WA 98127
For more information go to: www.fannypress.com
alexcuckoldstories.fannypress.com

This is a work of fiction. Names, characters, places, brands, media, and incidents are either the product of the author's imagination or are used fictitiously.

Cover design by Sabrina Sun

The Education of a Cuckold: A Story of Love, Lust, and Fate
Copyright © 2013 by Alex Hathaway

ISBN: 978-1-60381-544-4 (Trade Paper)
ISBN: 978-1-60381-545-1 (eBook)

Printed in the United States of America

Acknowledgments

I WOULD LIKE TO offer a special thanks to those in my life who have given me an unflinching view of their sexual experiences, with and without me. Those honest views have allowed me to write stories that hopefully not only entertain the reader, but also contain the spark of truth and the intensity of self-discovery.

Also by the Author

From Housewife to Cuckoldress:

How I Took Sexual Control of a
Marriage in Crisis

Prologue

—

WE TALK ABOUT LOVE as a perk of maturity, something you can't fully experience until you are old enough. I met the love of my life when I was eighteen. Of course, if you think "love of my life" means we locked eyes and lived happily after, well, that's not the story I have to confess. But you'll know soon enough—if I can find the guts to type these secrets.

Chapter 1

BETH WAS DIFFERENT. I knew it when I first laid eyes on her. I was in high school in Charlotte, North Carolina, where all the girls had sexy eyes, southern drawls, and plenty of attitude. Beth had been voted "best ass in school" when she was a sophomore, but that's not really fair. She was so much more than that. Yeah, Beth did have an animal grace about her, a tanned flow from head to toe. Her body was made for sex. I was intimidated by her back then, even more so when she turned eighteen. Her breasts were modest in size, but at eighteen, Beth acted and looked like a full-grown woman. She always had these hunks from the swim team buzzing around her. I figured she was getting laid all the time.

We had a photography class together. As the senior student photographer, I was the teacher's assistant. I was always looking for a way to get to know Beth better. Beth knew me, but maybe not. I felt as if she saw right through me. I wasn't a bad looking guy, but I was on the short side and more of a bookworm than an athlete. I tried to stay in shape but I was hardly a swim hunk. I needed a different way to get her attention.

The opportunity came in a strange way. I was one of the first in school to get my hands on an mp3 player—this was before iPods came along. One Friday, I saw Beth sitting alone in the back, fiddling with her camera with a distant look in her eyes. You could guess by her expression that it was "boy problems." I had a song I didn't think she had heard before … I sucked up my courage and told her she might like to check it out.

We stepped out behind the building, which had a small back porch perfect for illegal smoke breaks. I remember my heart pounding while she listened. Suddenly I had her all to myself, her browned skin reflecting the sun. I never wanted that song to end. It was called "Mad World." You might have heard a cover of it in the movie *Donnie Darko*. It evoked the kind of emo-loner pensiveness I was really into at the time.

She handed the music player back to me.

"That was one of the most beautiful things I've ever heard," she said. "Thank you. Do you want to go on a walk?".

The next hour was a blur. I can't remember exactly what we talked about that day. I know we shared secrets we had never told anyone. Me growing up with a single father. Her dad and his drinking. We walked behind the stadium, into the woods, around the gym, and eventually back to the school. By the time we circled back, we were holding hands.

I loved all the whispering around school. I felt like a prom king. When Beth got back together with the guy she'd told me about, it didn't really bother me. It felt like our bond was deeper. Some of my friends made fun of me about that. But I knew I was right.

I want to tell you realistically how our relationship developed, but it was less a succession of anecdotes and more of an evolution of feeling, the gradual uncovering of a pre-existing bond. I took to driving her home from school, and we never seemed to make it straight home. We'd stop in a park, walk along the river. Anything to avoid home and the problems awaiting us there. In the six months leading up to graduation, it felt like we spent all our free time together. Yeah, occasionally when I'd call, she wouldn't answer. I figured she was with her boyfriend, and I'd feel a tug of a kind of pain that has become terribly familiar in the years since. But a day or two later, she'd always call.

I only kissed her once, just a peck one night when she was a bit tipsy, but I didn't worry about it. The fact that we would soon be kissing, having sex actually, seemed inevitable. I wasn't in a rush at all. Some of my friends got frustrated; they tried to get me to date other girls who had crushes on me. I wasn't interested. She was the one.

It was only when prom night arrived that I realized my predicament. I never admitted to myself how much I wanted Beth to go with me—until the night arrived. I knew she had already agreed to go with Brad, one of the "swim dorks," as the misfits I hung out with called them—that is, when we didn't call them worse.

I did find someone to go with me, a woman named "Deb" who was also on the swim team. Deb was a little scary. She was pretty good looking, but damn was she "available." Looking back, I know that Deb was just a girl who hadn't found her way in life yet. Spreading her legs was how she got by. I guess we took advantage of that. I didn't want to go alone, and she was a nice person as well as someone who might be into something sexual that night.

When prom night finally arrived, I got distracted by Beth and Brad. At one point I saw them slow dancing, and a surge of jealousy blasted through. Deb could see that something was wrong. I wasn't my usual wisecracking self. At the after party, I found Beth outside on the patio making out, Brad lying on top of her. I felt an unwanted sexual thrill watching them writhe around in plain view.

Deb seemed annoyed by my inattention, at one point asking me what was wrong.

Later, while I was trying to keep an eye on Beth's make-out session, Deb tapped me on the shoulder.

"Jason …" I barely heard her first request.

"Jason!" she tapped me on the shoulder.

That time I turned around.

"I got a ride home with Becky…" Deb said.

"Okay," I said, a bit absentmindedly. I didn't mean to be rude to her. I was just so wrapped up in what was going on with Beth.

"You really need to get over her!" Deb said in disgust and walked off.

Ugh. There was a break in the music right when she said it, and our friends overheard her. Being called out by Deb was an unpleasant reminder that my feelings for Beth were at best unconventional. For the first time it occurred to me there might be something wrong with me, something abnormal. That's the last thing a high school student ever wants to feel.

I stormed out of the party, making sure to make enough of a scene that Beth knew I was upset. I drove out of town, pretending I was hitting the open road like my heroes Jack Kerouac and Hunter Thompson. But that was not my life. I was in my mom's beat-up Toyota Camry, and she needed it for work the next day. After I got an hour out of town, I could see less neon, and the exits were fewer and farther apart. Nothing to do but turn around.

I slid the keys on the plant shelf outside my mom's bedroom, then proceeded to cry my way to sleep.

But a few hours later, I woke up.

And for the first time, I masturbated, not thinking of myself having sex, but of my "girlfriend"—if I could still call her that with any sense of self-respect—having sex with another guy.

Beth didn't call the next day, or the day after that. At first I could barely eat. The second day was worse. On the third, she called.

"I heard you left the party all wrecked out," she said.

"Yeah …"

"I … I was in a whole other world," she said. "Sorry I wasn't there for you."

I didn't say anything, letting the silence be my weapon.

Finally I had mercy on her.

"It's okay. I had some things I had to reckon with." I always talked like that back then, portraying my existential battles as some kind of glorious struggle.

"What did you do?"

"I went on a long drive, got my head straight," I said.

"That's good," she said. "You still sound kind of weird though …"

Things felt really awkward. No! I couldn't let this fall apart. I had to bridge the gap.

"But as you know, I'm pretty tilted to begin with," I said.

We laughed, more out of relief. Things would be okay. That comfortable bond eased its way back.

After we hung up, I was a little troubled. Then I realized what was bothering me: I had never flat-out told her how I felt about her. There was no way around it. But not until after graduation. I wanted to get my courage up. Plus I didn't want to be forced to see her every day if it all fell flat.

Graduation was bittersweet. My friends were heading to colleges up and down the East Coast. I had a decent scholarship myself. Things were looking up. College would bring new adventures, not to mention hot girls. I threw my graduation cap as high as I could. If anything was going to stop me, in that moment I couldn't think of it.

I was feeling brazen, so I figured I'd roll with it. Asking Beth to go on a walk down by the sand dunes suddenly felt like nothing. We held hands as we always did. It was hard not to think about her white summer skirt floating against her strong, fit body. I fought off an image of swimdork Brad peeling it off her as I desperately wanted to do.

I sat Beth down on a bench and I took the plunge. I said I had always loved her, that I couldn't explain why or how. The cockiness left me—I felt like I was falling. Maybe that's why I didn't say everything I had planned; I didn't know how. It was all I could do to lay it all out there. But I did it. I could see her eyes well up as she clutched my hand.

Then she pulled me to her and kissed me. It was a moment I had built up beyond fairness. Now that it had arrived, I was the one confused. *It wasn't everything I had expected.* Maybe it was my insecurities, or maybe she was holding something back. We walked back from the dunes, still holding hands, but quiet. As we got closer to her house, she pulled her hand away.

I wanted to light up that spark in her that would make her run to me, but how? We said an awkward but emotional goodbye. I drove into the night, pushing the speed limit, wondering how I would find a way out of this "almost" situation. It was thrilling, yes, but it was also humiliating. Then, a terrifying thought flashed in and out. *The humiliation was a little thrilling also.* I couldn't hold that in my head for more than a second—my high school brain couldn't handle it. Anyhow, I knew I could triumph over those feelings if I could just get her to love me, to want me.

I felt a sudden urge to get away before all of this came to a head. I had a couple friends who were making a go of it in Fort Lauderdale, why not get the hell out of here? They had already asked me down there. All I had to do was get permission from my folks and find a way down.

I ran. Or to be more precise, I pooled my meager restaurant wages and got on a plane. I didn't do it to break Beth's heart or make her want me more. I did it because I had played every card in my hand. After that day of confessions, seeing her would make me search compulsively for another move I didn't have. So I went to Florida to make a life, or at least a summer.

Chapter 2

—————

WE DIDN'T TALK MUCH while I was gone. I didn't call her. Somehow I willed myself to leave her alone. She called me a couple times, but she seemed nervous, distant, maybe even a little angry. As if I had abandoned her. Summer flew by, and college was coming. I didn't get laid that summer, but the beach, the bonfire parties—all those irresponsible nights you miss like crazy when you get older—those were more than enough.

Finally it was time for me to go back home and pick up my stuff. My mother had already moved out of the house, relocating to Los Angeles in pursuit of professional dreams she had put on hold for me. I could only cheer her on after all the double shifts she had worked. The new buyer was ready to move in, waiting for me to clean out my room and drop off the key. It felt hollow to pack my childhood in boxes. This place I called home was over. As I taped up the last couple of boxes, the tears welled.

The next problem was finding somewhere to stay for the next couple of weeks until college began. I did have a fall back option, though it wasn't one I particularly wanted. Beth had an extra room at her place. To this day, a part of me wonders why I didn't try harder to find a buddy's couch. I guess I just missed her. Or maybe I craved what was about to happen. At any rate it was a fork in the road and boy did I take it. Calling her about a place to stay was a relief for both of us, a reason to talk besides the hard stuff. Beth agreed quickly. She seemed so happy that I was immediately glad about the decision.

I haven't mentioned Beth's sister yet, but she enters into this story prominently. Beth's sister Jamie was six years older than her. Jamie had such a wild child reputation that even six years out of high school, people still talked about the crazy things she did, or supposedly did. Sex with a teacher (albeit after she graduated and was of legal age) was just one of the stories that trailed her.

Jamie had a different thing going than Beth. Beth was shorter, smaller breasted. Jamie was taller with full breasts and long blond hair (Beth generally wore hers shorter). Jamie was your classic heartbreaker, the kind of girl I would never think of approaching. She was a few inches taller than me in height and had tons of "I'm out of your league" attitude. But it was worse. Jamie was one of those women I always felt could see right through me. She was so cocky in how she moved through the world. It was like she could see every motivation behind my social façade. To tell the truth I felt naked in front of her. She was terrifying. Much later in life, when I explored the fetish world, I realized that Jamie was what you would call a "natural Domme." As far as I know, she had never participated in BDSM subculture, but she seemed to understand the weaknesses of men as well as any Domme a submissive man might conjure. She was a Praying Mantis.

I wasn't sure what Jamie thought of me back then, but I knew she didn't look upon me with much fondness. Once when I came to see Beth late at night, I came through the back door and startled Jamie in the kitchen. Her response: "Stalk much?" For the last couple of years, Jamie had been living at home again, helping to run her dad's telecommunications business. She was living in the garage apartment, but it had a bridge into the main house. Sometimes if I was up late with Beth, Jamie would surprise us by coming in from the bridge stairs and raiding the kitchen. Maybe I was paranoid, but she always seemed to be hiding a mocking smile when she was around me, as if she was cruelly thinking, "You don't have a chance with Beth."

A few days into my stay at Beth's house, all the dominos fell. I was supposed to be out all night at my buddy Neil's party. Beth had to work—or so I thought. She was a waitress at Friendly's, pulling in a few bucks. Plans went awry; Neil's parents got wind of the party and shut it down early. After knocking softly as usual, I came in the back door of Beth's house and went into the kitchen. Jamie was there, spooning out of a pint of ice cream.

There were also empty beers cans on the counter. Jamie was known to suck a few drinks down. Alcohol tended to make her even less inhibited—if that was possible. Beth had told me a story once that I wasn't sure I could believe about Jamie and an ex-boyfriend who had cheated on her. She had allegedly sucked down a six pack and then fucked his arch-rival right in front of him at a party. It was one of those legends that followed her around but without sticking to her like it would most girls.

"Uh-oh," Jamie said when I came in, looking at me real funny.

"What?"

"Well, maybe it's just as well." With a knowing smile, she added, "Come with me. I think it will be better to, uh, show you."

I had never been all the way down the narrow hallway where Jamie led me, beyond the guest rooms her family maintained. Toward the end was a basement room their doctor father had turned into a private den, his own sterile version of a man cave. Turns out the girls used it as their "make out room," sneaking boys into the house whenever he was out of town, or even sometimes when their parents were asleep. There was a back staircase to the den that for some reason had never been completed. It led to a landing the family used for storage, where the boxes were piled high.

Jamie turned off the hall light and quietly opened the door to the landing area, pressing a finger to her lips to shush me. As she opened the door I heard the unmistakable sounds of sex.

It was dark behind the boxes, but Jamie pulled me over to a section that was opened up a little. The boxes had been stacked in a way to allow someone to peer between them and get a good look at the sprawling, half-finished room below. Jamie pulled me over and pointed my head down toward the opening for a good view.

"Brace yourself," she whispered grimly.

I looked through the opening and saw Beth kneeling down about twenty feet away. She was sucking on the biggest cock I had ever seen. I hadn't seen that many erect cocks, probably just my own and a few in pornos. This one was bigger, and it was black. With hindsight I realize now it was hardly a gargantuan penis, but it was the biggest I had seen. Beth was stroking it with both hands. No, she wasn't just stroking it; she was sucking on it with abandon. Her hips were rotating as she kneeled, almost like she was in heat. Her gorgeous naked ass was moving around everywhere, as if in search of an invisible cock to fill it immediately.

I felt a piercing betrayal unlike any I had known, albeit an irrational one. After all, Beth had never promised me anything romantically or sexually other than a tentative kiss I naively took as a promise.

"That's a big cock, isn't it?" Jamie whispered into my ear.

"Beth's been fucking it for the last two hours at least. If you'd come in earlier, you would have heard her screams in your guest room."

Kneeling on the carpet squares in front of the sofa, Beth

was saying something to the guy and staring up at him in admiration—a different kind of admiration than she had accorded me.

I heard the guy laugh as he reached for his pants, fished out a fresh condom, and handed it to Beth, who unwrapped it.

"That's Billy," Jamie said. "Billy and I used to date. I got him and Beth introduced earlier this summer, and she's been thanking me ever since."

I was speechless.

Jamie continued, "She begged me to stay up late tonight so if you got home early you wouldn't run into them. She knows she should have waited until you left town, but she just couldn't wait. She really needed to fuck."

As if on cue, Beth was rolling the condom over Billy's penis. It looked like she was struggling to stretch it over the thickness. Once the condom was pushed up pretty far, Beth did something that really surprised me. With some urgency, she moved over to the edge of the couch and stuck her "best in school" ass in the air, held her hips up to him, and begged Billy to fuck her.

Billy eased his big penis inside her, clearly enjoying the sight of her round ass begging for him like that. I was assuming it would be difficult for a big cock like that to get inside an eighteen-year-old like Beth, but she didn't appear to be having too much difficulty. She started making a happy meowing sound when he was just hallway in. All the same, Billy moved in and out slowly, letting her get used to the rhythm.

"This is why I wanted you to come down here," whispered Jamie. "The girls in our family—we all started having sex when we were pretty young, and we cover for each other."

I watched the action in an improbable trance, with this "out of my league" blond goddess behind me whispering in my ear. It was like I had been fast-forwarded and dropped in the middle of a terrifying horror movie. My ego was in shock.

"I wanted you to see Beth like this, because you've been

trying to get in her pants for what, a year I think, right?"

I was glad Jamie couldn't see my face, which flashed red.

"Get this: Beth fucked Billy the first night they met."

Billy was moving in and out a little faster now, getting into a groove with his thrusting. It didn't look to me like he was all the way in yet, maybe halfway. Recalling the scene now, I believe his big dick was probably about eight inches long, a perfect size for a standing doggy-style fuck. Plenty of length to move in and out without actually slipping out.

"So you see," Jamie snarled, "You really need to let Beth go, because it's not working out. *She's not spreading for you.*"

I guess you can see now why I think Jamie would have been a natural with a bullwhip and a man crawling on his knees. She just *knew*.

Jamie had been resting her right hand on a box near my head. She moved it down for a different angle and ended up brushing over the tent in my pants.

"Oh, I see you enjoy the show," she laughed in hushed whispers, rubbing her hand over my crotch. "I don't blame you," she cooed. "Watching Beth get it on is … pretty awesome."

She rubbed the outside of my pants in vague circles. I was all the way hard, straining against my zipper, feeling *so* out of control.

Jamie gave me a squeeze through my pants. I felt a jolt of sensation as I watched Beth start to move her hips in circles, getting into a groove with Billy. My only sexual experiences up to this point had been awkward—fun, but awkward. Beth and Billy were nothing like awkward. They were completely in tune, like two well-practiced dance partners.

Jamie worked my zipper, feeling her way into my boxers. From there she easily pulled me out through the opening; I could feel the breeze on my dick as she continued to stroke it.

"Now, doesn't that feel good?" Jamie whispered in my ear.

But then came the words that changed everything:

"*Oh!* Your little dick likes it! Likes watching my sister get fucked while I stroke it."

I had fooled around with five girls, had sex with a couple of them. No one had ever taken charge of me like this, and no one had ever called my dick small. It was humiliating.

"*I just knew you had a tiny dick,*" Jamie hissed triumphantly. "Little-dicked guys are always chasing girls like my sister around, trying to be nice to her, calling her too much, buying her concert tickets ..." That last one hurt, because I had bought Beth tickets to several concerts over the years, even when I couldn't go with her.

"And yeah, she talks to you for hours on the phone ... *but only after she's been fucked.*"

"Watch her get fucked!" Jamie whispered more loudly as she stroked her fingers up and down my cock. I had stroked myself off plenty of times, but never felt this kind of sensation.

As Jamie picked up her intensity, Beth and Billy did too. With a harsh thrust he pulled back both her arms and jammed his cock all the way up in her—no more half thrusts.

"Oh wow!" You could hear Beth easily now. "Wow!"

Billy was getting cockier with each thrust. "That's what you wanted, isn't it bitch?"

"Oh god, yes!" Beth said with abandon. "That feels so good!" The few times I called Beth a bitch we had gotten into fights. But when Billy said it, she seemed to love it.

"You ready to get your pussy fucked, you fucking slut?"

"Oh please!" Beth begged. I had never seen her beg for anything, or let a guy talk to her like this. But she begged for more, looking back to spur him on with an expression on her face I will never forget. *Because I had never seen that expression before.* Regardless of all the secrets we had shared, there were some she wouldn't share with me. And here she was, desperate to share them with Billy. No, rather, he *took* them from her.

Billy pounded her savagely. I had never heard such obscene sounds, like she was being plunged from the inside, her ass slapping up against him. Her legs were trembling and he had to prop up her waist to keep her from collapsing.

Like Billy, Jamie was feeling her power. "You like it, don't you? You like me jerking your little cock while you watch my sister get fucked."

"Yes!" I said helplessly, strangely comfortable in Jamie's power, though scared of what she might do to me.

"A little surprised, aren't you? Surprised she'd give up her pussy like that?"

"Yeah," I admitted, still in a trance, eyes riveted to the scene.

"That's what girls do. We're can't help ourselves with a guy like Billy. Look!"

Beth was screaming and sweating. You could see her legs shaking from top to bottom, violently to the point where you might have thought she was having a seizure.

"You like that, bitch?"

"Oh god I love it, Billy! Your dick is so big!!"

"You needed this fuck, didn't you?" he said, slamming into her, seeming to know the exact speed she needed.

"Oh god, yes, you fuck me so well!"

Billy stopped thrusting, just holding her deep, pulling her impossibly gorgeous ass up against him. I realized he was doing it to absorb her spasms. It was amazing to watch her ass shake and cum all over his cock. She may have been shy about kissing me, but I had to accept she knew how to fuck. This was hardly her first time.

"You wish you were him," Jamie said sexily in my ear. "You wish you were him making her scream like that right now … Don't you?"

"Yes," I said helplessly. She increased the pace of her stroking. I realized with some embarrassment I was going to cum soon; I couldn't help myself. It was probably a miracle I had held on as long as I did.

By now, Beth and Jamie had slowed their pace, and she was doing most of the work. He stood there with his hands behind his head, smiling like a bandit as she desperately pushed her ass up and onto him.

"That's it, my little slutgirl, come get this cock you love …" Billy taunted her. Beth just moaned and backed up.

"You wish you could treat her like that … make her desperate to fuck you like that," Jamie whispered savagely in my ear."

"Yes …" I said again, breathing more heavily. A diabolical, red hot sex thought was dawning on me, aided by Jamie's stroking: much as I loved Beth, much as I adored her, *I would have traded all that to make her feel the way she felt right now just once*, to make her cum like she had with Billy … like she was cumming again, right now. Billy just stood there, relaxing, while Beth screamed and pushed her ass all over his cock. Without even doing any work, any thrusting, he had brought her to another orgasm, her beautiful ass shaking with happiness.

Jamie could tell I was about to cum. "Don't yell when you shoot. You don't want her to know you're up here, being such a dirty boy," she whispered. Jamie was stroking me aggressively now. She had total control.

"Squirt little dick, squirt!" And so, with the hands of Beth's big sister clasped over my mouth, I squirted against a cardboard box while the girl I loved got her brains fucked out. *How was this happening?* I passed quickly from ecstasy to an unfamiliar shame. Beth stood up. I thought they were done, so I turned to leave, my post-orgasmic relief reminding me I had no business here.

"Wait … they're not done yet," I heard Jamie whisper from behind as she continued to caress and stroke my balls. "He's going to make her cum again, even harder. Just watch." Jamie had figured out something I didn't know … yet. When girls cum that hard, they usually have an even harder cum waiting.

Beth was standing up against Billy, whispering in his ear and stroking his big cock. It halfway limp and running down her thigh, the condom still partly on. Watching her work her right hand up and down that arrogant shaft made me start to twitch again, but there was more. She wrapped her arms around him and starting kissing him, her hips smooshed up against his lanky strong body. He wasn't muscle-bound or even lean like the swim guys, but there was something about him—a total confidence that unsettled me even from here.

The passion of their embrace was startling. It was harder to watch this than the fucking had been. At least the fucking was impersonal; I could write it off as animalistic cravings. But this … this was intimate.

"See, that's how you make a girl love you," Jamie said. And then she said something shocking that has cursed and haunted me ever since. *"Once you own her pussy, her heart will follow."* She rubbed my balls gently, letting the words sink in. In less than a half hour, Jamie—on a six pack of beer—had utterly dismantled me. Afraid to go for the sexual jugular as guys like Billy did, I had conned myself into thinking I could "go sensitive," take care of a girl emotionally. Win her heart, and her body would follow.

But while you worked your game for a year, Billy owned her pussy the first night they met. Jamie's nasty voice rang in my head. It was harsh, but it made my cock twitch.

"Oh yeah," Jamie cooed, "You really like this," she said triumphantly. Crap, I was already hard again, already back into the scene. My whole "take the high road" romantic girl-chasing-game had been exposed as the desperate stalker-like charade I knew it was, deep down. And Jamie had always known. I could blame her for being mean, but was it mean to expose the farce behind my nice guy persona? Or was she doing the world a favor? In all the years since that improbable night, I have debated that question in my head. In that moment the debate was less important than the fallout; the consequences would be severe, but there was no time for that now. Beth pushed Billy back on the card table, leaning over and jacking his cock as it strained toward a full erection again. I could see her cooing nasty things to him but I couldn't make out the words.

Beth got up and pushed Billy onto the carpet, his cock sticking obscenely up in the air. She straightened out the condom so that it covered most of his cock again and eagerly mounted him. It was amazing to see his cock disappear inside her as her pussy strained to receive him. I was fascinated by a cock big enough to make it really difficult for a girl to sit down on it, and I wondered what that must feel like. I had only been inside a girl a few times and when she was riding me it was not at all difficult for her to get my cock inside her.

"Oh that feels good," Jamie said, as if responding to my thoughts. "That feels *really* good, having a man stretch you out like that. It's nothing you would know about, is it?" She was working me back up to rock hard once again.

Beth was done being quiet. "God I love your big black dick!" she goaded Billy, her back muscles rippling. As she started riding him hard, I could see the advantages of a longer cock: she could work her pussy all around his shaft without slipping out. Meanwhile, Billy could just relax, help her out with some casual thrusting. The one time I'd had sex in that position, I had struggled to stay inside the girl. Billy was giving Beth intense friction, and without much effort.

This was a great position for Beth because she didn't have to worry about controlling anything. Her weight provided a natural resistance. Each time she landed on him, she didn't take him all the way in—only as much as her body weight could handle. It seemed like she was cumming almost continuously, trembling, losing control, letting Billy take over the thrusting when she needed a break, sweat dripping down her back. When they fucked hard, you could hear the nasty squelching noises of a very filled up pussy.

Jamie seemed to sense me tensing up; she moved in for the kill. "You like watching Beth fuck, don't you?" she teased, expertly stroking me while whispering in my ear. "Don't you?!"

"Yes …" I whispered helplessly, almost too loud. The girl I loved was getting seen to by an expert right in front of me, and I couldn't have been more turned on. It hurt like hell watching her slipping away from me like that; it would sting even more later. But for now …

"You love it; your little dick loves it!" Jamie whispered triumphantly. "Get used to it. Girls love fucking big dicks!" By way of illustration, Beth surged even higher on Billy's cock, bouncing violently. Watching her move with such passion, with Jamie stroking me from behind, was just too much to take. I spurted helplessly in Jamie's hand as I watched Beth scream and twitch and thrust like a madwoman.

"That's it," Jamie said soothingly, cruelly. She leaned over me, her breasts landing comfortably on my back through her shirt while she looked over at my shoulder.

Beth seemed to be done fucking for now. She lifted her ass up, forcing Billy's cock out with a loud plop. Then she leaned over and kissed him, lovingly, soulfully. I hated that he knew how to be sweet to her afterwards. Savage, then sweet. That made the implications so much worse. She kissed him again, then laid herself down on his chest. He wrapped his arms around her and ran his fingers through her hair.

Jamie pulled at me from behind. "We should get out of here. Now that they aren't screwing they might hear us up here."

I zipped up and Jamie pulled me into the back hallway, pointing me toward the end of the hall. I found the door to the backyard and walked out through the wooden gate. I wouldn't return until well after midnight.

Chapter 3

———

I SPENT MOST OF the night walking around, head full of crazy thoughts about what I had just seen. When I came back, all the lights were out. I made my way to bed through the glow of the moon.

What happened the next day is hard to write about, even today, though I have masturbated while recalling the incident many times. When I manage to focus in on the sex, the emotional violence fades.

I slept in, hoping that Jamie would have gone to work and maybe Beth as well. I lay in bed, thinking about finding somewhere else to crash. I was torn between getting the hell out and unspeakable desires. I guess I hoped it was just a terrible wet dream. I think that was fair, given I have never experienced a scene like that in all the years since, even when I looked for it.

I still could not believe the sexual screams from this girl I had put on a pedestal. I started stroking again. Then: a knock on the door. It was Jamie and Beth. Beth was wearing these tight cutoffs she sometimes tortured the world with, along with an old Ramones t-shirt. Jamie had on a sundress that clung dangerously to her body. It was a lot of estrogen for anyone, much less a guy stroking himself under the covers. I quickly moved my hands away before they came in, hoping they wouldn't make the connection, though my cock twitching under the covers wasn't a big help.

Beth had a strange look on her face. Jamie meanwhile looked like she had more evil plans in store. I sat up in the bed, suddenly vulnerable.

"Jason," Jamie said, "do you have something to tell Beth?"

"About what"? I asked, worried about where she was going with this.

"About … last night."

I didn't know what to say. Everything seemed to be happening in slow motion.

"Is it true?" Beth asked. "Did you really, you know, *watch* me?"

I was taken off guard.

"Yes," I said with some resignation. So this was Jamie's end game. She had twisted her particular knife perfectly.

"Jamie told me all about it," Beth said. She looked hurt and angry—which I had seen a couple times before—but there was something else in her aspect I had not seen before, something unexpected: she was taking charge … of me.

"I'll leave the two of you to … talk," Jamie said, a wicked gleam in her eye.

Jamie closed the door and left the two of us, the best of friends, completely reassessing each other.

"Jamie told me … everything." Beth said, standing over the bed. I was in shock. I didn't have time to think about why Jamie would have exposed me like this.

"I can't believe that after how much we trusted each other, you would watch me … watch me fuck!"

She was disapproving, restless. There was no love in her eyes, but maybe there was a bit of sex.

"She even told me how horny it made you. It made you horny to watch me fuck?"

I was completely taken aback by her forcefulness. This wasn't like her at all.

"Didn't it?!"

"Yes," I admitted weakly.

"Jamie told me everything, and I mean *everything*," Beth said. "Do you know what that means?"

"I'm not sure," I said, fearing what she would say next.

"That means … she told me that she jerked your cock to two orgasms watching me fuck. Is that true?"

"Yes," I said, relieved. Close call.

"She said you were unbelievably hard watching the girl you supposedly love fuck someone else. I couldn't believe it!" Beth said. "I couldn't figure out why the hell you weren't down there fighting for my honor. There could only be a few reasons: one, that you didn't love me the way you say. But I thought, 'That can't be it.' "

Beth fiddled with one of the buttons in her cutoffs absentmindedly, giving me a view of her sun-browned stomach. She leaned over the edge of the bed and continued, "So then I was thinking, 'Well, he must have been afraid to get his ass kicked. After all, Billy is definitely much stronger.' But no, I've seen you play soccer and you throw yourself into much bigger guys all the time."

Beth leaned over farther. "So there's only one other possibility; you must have a small penis. That kind of thing can make a guy real … shy. I know that from experience."

Beth looked at me wickedly, with a touch of a smile, but a steely one. Her trademark warmth was nowhere to be seen. I didn't know what to say. I had never seen her like this. *Like she owned me.* Who was this girl I thought I had known so well?

"Let's see," Beth said, grabbing for my sheet. I instinctively pulled it back, but she pulled harder, and down it went. I wasn't even hard anymore; my cock had retreated into a protective shell.

"Yes! Just as I thought," Beth said. "Guys with little dicks are such a pain."

I didn't know what to say. The history of our intimate friendship reduced to this humiliation.

"Let me get that little dick hard," Beth said, straddling me. "I want to show you something." She moved her crotch up and down my groin area; the pressure made for intense sensations. I started to get hard looking up at her, swaying over me in her cutoffs, totally in control.

"Does that feel good?" Beth said.

"Oh god ..." was all I could muster.

"Yeah, that does feel good," Beth said, rubbing herself on me, grinding on me through her shorts, her brown ass jutting out of her cutoffs in the sexiest way you could imagine.

"You should imagine what my pussy feels like from the inside," Beth cooed at me. "It's so wet, so warm."

I was already rock hard.

Beth sat up and fondled my erection.

"I still can't believe you watched me," she said. "What were you thinking?"

Silence.

"You know how creepy that is?"

I was going to say something about her sister watching her not being such a classy move either, but I thought better of it.

"We're supposed to be friends," Beth said. *"You're supposed to have my back!"*

I felt ashamed, dirty. But I was harder than ever. I worried that I was going to spurt on Beth's shirt. Something told me that was not going to improve the situation at all. Jamie had really set me up! She must despise me ...

"So I want you to at least be honest with me," Beth said, stroking me a bit more intensely. "Did you like watching me fuck?"

Ugh.

"I said, did you like watching me fuck!?" Beth almost shouted, and I got red-faced, wondering if Jamie could hear.

"Yes."

"Did you like watching my pussy cum on that big cock?"

"Yes," I said, helplessly. There was no use denying it.

"I'll bet you didn't know I was such a slut, did you?"

I was surprised to hear her use that word about herself.

"No."

"Well, I am," Beth said, stroking me faster.

"We're all sluts … to guys who can fuck as well as Billy."

"Actually, it's a relief to tell you how much I love to fuck. I really hated pretending. And I hated lying to you or making excuses when I needed to get my pussy taken care of."

With that, Beth got up.

"Where are your condoms?" she asked aggressively.

I was slow to respond, so she brazenly opened up the top dresser drawer where I kept most of my clothes.

Before I could say anything, she had rummaged around and found a box. She pulled at the tape. The package was a bit worn but still unopened.

"Unused … that's no surprise," she said, laughing. Where did this mean girl come from and would Beth ever come back to me? If I wasn't so aroused I would have cried.

Beth pulled a condom out and before I knew it, she was putting it on my cock. I could see the cleavage from her small but very firm breasts poking out as she leaned over.

"Get up!" she said in such a tone of command I had no choice but obey.

As I stared at her in a stupor, Beth peeled down her cutoffs, then her t-shirt, practically throwing it off. Her panties came next, teasing down her legs. She hopped onto the bed and lay back, spreading her legs wantonly, rubbing between them with her fingers.

"C'mon, this is what you've wanted all this time, right? Get on top of me and fuck the shit out of me!!!"

Was I living a dream or a nightmare? She was right—I'd wanted this for the longest time—but not like this. *Not like this!* I was thinking passionate kisses, tender caresses, whispers of affection. All the intimate things that would have given me a strength I could count on. But I felt vulnerable … naked.

"Let's go!" she said impatiently.

Not wanting to humiliate myself further, I got on the bed, kneeled near her. I tried to ignore that voice in my mind warning me that I was practically a virgin, that I didn't know what I was doing. What was worse, my cock wasn't even all the way hard anymore.

I struggled to get the condom on my half-hard dick. I felt the beginnings of hot tears in my eyes and tried like crazy to suppress them.

Fortunately Beth came to the rescue of my self-esteem, expertly unwrapping the condom and in the process getting my dick harder through her touch as she worked the condom up on my dick. I felt so self-conscious as I lined my cock up with her pussy. I tried to find my way inside her.

"Get it in there!" Beth demanded as she put her elbows up to see what was going on. Her tanned brown thighs looked incredible, keeping me horny and not just terrified. I tried to push myself inside her. I wasn't getting anywhere with it though. Goddamnit! This was turning into a nightmare.

Beth saw how stressed out I was and had pity.

"I'll help with that," she said, and grabbed my cock. She lined it up easily and without even looking, pulled me forward. I was in! There was a moment of tightness, then I was inside her.

"Oh!" Beth said. I started to get excited, feeling the pleasure for both of us. Nothing had ever felt as incredible as all her warmth around my dick.

"That's it," Beth said, pulling my ass toward her. "Give it to me."

I did, pushing in pretty hard, looking down to make sure

I didn't come all the way out. This was going to take some practice. I didn't want to get too crazy and slip out. That much I knew about sex with girls from my few prior misadventures.

"C'mon Jason, give it to me! This is what you wanted, right?"

"Right!" I said, eager to please her.

Now that the initial tightness was gone, I started giving it to her harder.

"Give it to me," Beth said. Then, pulling her supple legs around me, she added more coolly, "Give it to me harder."

I pounded her harder. That seemed to work. Each time I hit the base of her pussy I could tell she could feel it better.

I thrust at a rapid rate, doing my best to please her. But when she worked her ass up toward me, the rhythm got more complicated. I fell out. She quickly pulled me back in, but it kept happening. The next two times, it wasn't as easy to pull me inside. The rhythm was broken. She didn't hide her frustration.

"Your little cock keeps falling out. Just when it gets good, it falls out." She glared at me with impatience. "Try to keep it in there and pound me."

I did my best, but now I was getting nervous and falling out more often. Tears welled up again but I fought them off, sensing she would have no sympathy for me now.

"Slow it down," Beth said. "It's better for you to go slower and not fall out as much."

So I went slower, and that helped. I was moving in and out without the slippage, getting into a decent rhythm. Beth lay back with her legs spread wide, trying to keep the rhythm simple for me.

"See, that's the other problem with little dicks," Beth said. "I can't feel a thing. See how easy it is to work it in me?"

I nodded, embarrassed.

"With Billy's dick, pretty much every time he pushes it in me, it hurts … but *so* good." Then the clincher, driven home with all her resentment, "*You wanted to fuck me—but you can't.*"

I tried to fuck her better but it just made her laugh out loud.

"All this time, you wanted to get in this pussy, and your dick was too small to begin with." I could not believe her cruelty. *But more than that, I could not believe how right it felt.* Then I had a horrible/amazing thought I have never, ever forgotten. *Finally, some truth between the two of you after all this BS about "how close we are."* The shame made my dick rock hard, the words to "Cruel to be Kind" rattled off in my head from somewhere.

I was fucking away while she trash-talked me. Hurt, mad, confused … horny.

"You couldn't help yourself so you watched."

"You stroked your little dick and watched me. You knew it was wrong but you couldn't help it."

"And now you're fucking me—kind of."

"Be careful what you wish for with that tiny dick!" With that she just burst out laughing and it took a big thrust from me to stop her pussy from expelling me completely. But then she pushed harder and I slipped right out, leading her to laugh hard enough to roll on her side.

My supposed best friend had no sexual mercy. Looking at her magnificent body, a thought long repressed burst out: *what right do you have to fuck her?* But then: *don't let it end like this!* I pushed her legs up forcefully inserted myself into her. But I was too worked up.

Before I knew it, I was twitching and cumming inside her.

Realizing that a brief, substandard fuck was all she was going to get from me, she started laughing again, completing my humiliation. This time I did let a couple tears fall, thinking it would break her cruel trance. But it didn't.

"Oh, a quick cummer too! Well that doesn't really surprise me."

Beth whipped my dick out of her, holding my condom by the base to prevent it from slipping off. She seemed to be paying a lot more attention to my condom that she had to Billy's last night. God she was experienced at sex. I felt like such a boy. Once I was out, the condom came off easily.

"That tiny dick was barely in that thing," Beth said. "We're lucky the condom didn't slip off you," she said.

I lay down beside her, reaching for her hand, but she pulled hers away, distracted.

"Dammit that was the worst fuck I've had in a long time," Beth said. I realized later that there is nothing more "cruel to be kind" than a hot girl who is restless with cum.

I was stunned.

"What are we going to do about that? Huh? There's no way you're going to fuck me to orgasm. We're going to have to try something else. Are you good with your tongue?"

"I think so," I said, not wanting to come off as utterly incapable.

"Well have you ever eaten a girl out?" Beth asked demandingly while sitting up in the bed.

I was going to lie and say yes, but something about the way she glared at me convinced me otherwise.

"No," I said.

"Okay, well, that's not going to work, I don't feel like teaching you how to eat pussy. Go ahead and finger me," she said. "Let's see how that goes."

With that, Beth propped herself up on a couple of pillows and patted down the space next to her. "Lie next to me and get me off," she said, still in her demanding tone.

I lay down next to her, rolling onto my side. I moved my fingers up her thigh, feeling my way into her pussy. I was really nervous. I had never done this before either, except once in a girl's jeans in the back of a movie theater, and that didn't really count; the stakes were not this high. I put my fingers in her cautiously, feeling the wetness suck me in. Leaning up against her rounded ass, I felt how amazing it was to be so close to her. I wanted to get her off more than anything, to reclaim a shred of sexual pride.

I just felt my way into her, trying to move my fingers in a nice rhythm.

She moaned. "Oh that feels good, Jason. Keep that going."

I worked my way in and out, adding an extra finger so I had three fingers moving. She moaned appreciatively so I added a fourth, and she moaned even louder. I could feel her pussy clenching harder now, harder than it had on my cock earlier.

I worked in a little deeper, not sure how rough I should be, but her moaning was getting stronger, so I was doing something right. I felt some sexual confidence returning when I realized I could sense her body's movements and respond to them. Maybe I could take her to orgasm after all.

But Beth had a different agenda. She pulled my hand out and rolled over, sitting back against the pillows. "Let me take it from here," Beth said. "Sit up so you can see this."

I sat up and watched as Beth starting working her right hand into her pussy, a couple of fingers dipping in and out. "Ohh …" she said as she closed her eyes. "When you're doing a girl with your fingers, find a way to work the clit." She moved her hand outside her pussy and rubbed her fingers teasingly up and down the sides of her clit and vaginal opening. "Just be careful. You don't have to touch the clit that much—it gets too intense—just work it till you feel the girl move …"

She was being sort of sweet to me again, but more like a stern teacher than a lover or a close friend. As she teased her clit, her legs started to move. I was entranced just watching her please herself.

"That's the next best thing to a great fuck—knowing how to work this. I can cum nice this way. Let me show you."

"Oh yeah," Beth said, opening her eyes for a moment to look down. She worked a couple of fingers inside with one hand while she rubbed on her clit with the other, sometimes pinching it gently. "You like watching this?" she asked.

"Yeah," I said.

"That's okay. Rub it for me, jerk it while I do. Let's cum together."

I stroked myself, instantly coming to life. Beth pulled her

legs closer together, applying more pressure as her hand stroked faster.

"Oh god," Beth said as her body tightened. She was rubbing feverishly now in short strokes. It dawned on me later that taking charge of me and cutting our lovemaking to the core must have turned her on as well. It was a raw display of power. Suddenly her legs clasped her hands and she almost rolled off her side of the bed from the intensity. "Oh yeah!!" I was taking feverish mental notes of the path to her ecstasy.

It was awesome to hear her happy moans, to somehow share this moment with her. She sounded so beautiful when she was cumming like that, all the problems in her life so far away.

She was in her zone for a minute or so. Then she finally rolled back over and looked at me. "Did you cum?" she asked.

"No," I said shyly. Nothing about this brutal adventure had really gone right for me. "I think, you know, because I had just cum ..."

"Oh no, I'm sure we can make you cum again," Beth said confidently.

With that she got up, kneeled next to me on the bed, and firmly reached for my cock, which was already almost hard. As soon as her hand touched it, it twitched and swelled even harder.

"Yeah, definitely more cum in here," Beth said, stroking me casually, sort of examining my dick with her hand. "You feel like cumming again?"

"Yeah," I said.

"Because I can make you cum harder than you have, probably ever," she said. The cocky way she looked at me, it was hard to doubt her. She wasn't really confident in the classroom, so I had no idea until now how incredibly confident she was in the bedroom, how confident she was as a woman.

"Want me to make that little dick cum?" she asked.

I twitched again, noticeably. I wished she hadn't said that again, but a part of me was thrilled as well.

"You like to be teased, don't you? Just like my sister said." Beth stroked me a bit faster. Then all of a sudden she pulled herself on top of me. I could feel her wet pussy juices on my thighs. She held my cock up against her belly, as if to take an eyeball measurement of it. She seemed to suppress another laugh.

"Such a dirty boy," Beth said, "such a dirty, LITTLE DICKED boy." She stroked and stared me down, daring me to contradict her. And there was no way I could. Her fingers felt sensational on my dick, so very different than my own. My erection was so hard that it actually hurt. The brutality of damaging our friendship for this sex made my pending orgasm all the more intense.

"God you feel so fucking small in my hand," she said.

I looked at her hand. It was true.

"My hand almost completely covers your tiny dick," she went on, amazed. "Jeez, with Billy even two hands aren't enough."

I flushed at the comparison.

"Well, maybe you're not all the way hard yet," she mused while stroking and taking a closer look. But that wasn't the case. With her muscular legs straddling me and her pussy tantalizing me on her thigh, I could not have been longer or harder.

"Yep, you're so hard for me," Beth said. "You must like my body." Still stroking with her right hand, she pulled at her breast with the other.

"Do you like it?" she asked me, giving me a manipulative flash of vulnerability.

"Yeah," I said.

"I can tell," she said, smiling at me. "I love that I turn you on so much."

She was stroking me firmly but slowly. Even so, I wouldn't last long. But I didn't want to cum. I didn't want this pleasure to end. *Nor did I want to face the life that awaited me after this orgasm.*

"Jason, did you dream about fucking me, dream about it for a long time?"

She stared at me, no longer looking angry. But she kept on stroking me.

"Yeah …" I said. It felt good to just tell her the truth, to stop pretending I was above lusting after her. The way she moved was so effortless. How many times had I stared at her as she walked off, or took a drag on a friend's cigarette?

"That's good … and that's why you were watching me last night, right?"

I was hesitant … but she kept stroking.

"God I love to fuck," Beth said. "Billy—the first time my sister introduced me to him, I knew he was going to be shoving his cock inside me. I didn't care if he had a girlfriend, I didn't care if it would hurt your feelings, I just had to fuck him. He looked at me like he could just split me open, take whatever he wanted …"

I had to try hard not to cum hearing her talk like this.

"And a few hours later, he did. God, he made me his slut!"

She started stroking me harder with her right hand while touching herself with her left.

"But then, you know that, because you saw us."

Silence.

"I'm glad you know," she continued. "I'm glad you know what a fucking whore I can be for a fuck like that. You probably thought was I some kind of angel, but I'm not. Well, sometimes I am. But other times I'm just a dirty girl who needs to cum on a big fat cock."

I wasn't going to be able take much more of this. I was twitching on the bed. I think she could tell, as she was working me faster, expertly.

"And you like to watch me, don't you? Don't you?!"

I couldn't help myself, so I just blurted out "Yes!"

Suddenly I was spurting again.

"Oh yeah, look at that little dick cum. Look at it!" She was triumphant.

I spasmed into her, amazed at the intensity of my orgasm. I didn't have a lot of cum left in me, so it was almost like dry heaves, but my whole body was writhing. It felt amazing.

Beth smiled, grabbed some Kleenex and wiped the drips.

"I wish you could see Billy cum up close," she said. "His big cock makes such a mess. I have to shower every time he spurts near me. You need a fucking beach towel to clean up after he squirts!"

She must have seen the flash of jealousy in my eyes and had some pity on me, because her voice softened and she lay down next to me, putting her arm across my chest.

"I guess we learned a lot about each other, huh?"

"Yeah," I said. I felt relaxed but I was probably in shock. Things were changing so fast.

When Beth told me she had to shower and go to work, I was almost relieved. As much as I enjoyed lying in her arms, I needed to get out of there.

As I watched her walk nude to the bathroom, I wondered if I would ever get to see her like that again. I was dizzy from how she had treated me. I snuck out the back hallway, wanting to avoid Jamie at all costs. I did not understand what had motivated Jamie's diabolical behavior and I did not want to risk further assaults on my ego.

It was only years later that I considered the possibility Jamie might have been driven not to annihilate me but to liberate me. A strange form of liberation … but I was free of some illusions after that incident, that much could not be denied.

The next day, I moved out. Jamie gave me a wicked look of understanding when I said goodbye, which gave me masturbation fodder for days to come. There was no sign of Beth. I was only left to wonder if I could recover any kind of status in her eyes as I shut the kitchen door behind me.

I felt a jolt of shame shoot through my body, as if the two

of them had exposed me for the depraved freak I had always been, the one I had fought so hard to deny through the "most popular rebel but treats girls classy" persona they had completely deconstructed. As I got on my bike and peddled off, I felt like a kid again, a kid with no future—certainly no future with a girl like Beth. The tears ran salty and hot. I had to stop a couple of times and wipe my eyes on my sweatshirt.

Chapter 4

——

I FOUND ANOTHER FRIEND I could stay with. I crashed on his couch in the stench of dirty water bongs, but it was worth the hassles of his friends partying all around me. Believe it or not, I spent the days missing Beth. I found myself torn between savoring the taboo sexual memories of what had happened and feeling bitterly disappointed in myself. I did manage enough dignity not to call her on the phone.

In the back of my mind not calling her gave me some satisfaction, as if I was punishing her. Though I had to question whether I had any emotional hold on her at all. Had Beth just played me for companionship? The only time it all made sense was when I was jacking off at the end of the day, reliving those scenes again and again. But after I orgasmed, the emotions would always come back. Waves of loneliness and inadequacy. I found myself wondering if I would ever talk to her again. Could I ever satisfy a woman? Would a girl ever love me enough to give me a chance to find out?

Fortunately for me, life always has some twists in store, and some of them are good. In just a few surreal days after I moved out of Beth's place, hopped on a Greyhound bus and was soon swept up in the adventure of college. The bus ride down to Atlanta was full of anticipation. And you know what? College was one of the few things where anticipation didn't let me down. I logged as many adventures as I could have hoped for, though not necessarily the exact ones I wanted. Looking back, it doesn't matter a bit. All the adventures feel like gold.

When you are partying into the night with dormitory pals from across the country, playing loud music, getting stoned, sharing your dreams about what life could be someday—well, it has a way of pushing some of the bad memories away. I started to get a glimpse of my former cockiness, which had been almost eradicated in those two days with Beth. It felt good to have it back.

I was relieved to see there wasn't any lasting damage to my self-esteem. Well, with the possible exception of one night stands. I found myself especially shy around a certain type of girl I would meet in college, one who was confident in her body and evaluating me primarily for sex. Not for a relationship, just a sexual frolic.

My first run-in with that kind of girl was during the first week of school, on a sunny day in the quad outside the dorms. This girl, Cassie, was wearing cut-off shorts and her legs were thick with muscle.

"You're staring at my legs, aren't you?" she asked, while looking me right in the eye. So much for small talk.

"So, what are you going to do about it?" was her next question. I mumbled something. I couldn't get away fast enough.

But there were plenty of girls who weren't just scoping guys out sexually. I learned there was a kind of friendship I could develop with a girl. Most times it led to sexual frustration and platonic relationships, but every now and then that friendship resulted in closeness and some sex.

There was a girl I met halfway through my first year, Sandy, who fit that bill. We only dated for three months, and we didn't really fall in love, but we "fell in like." Kissing her was the most natural thing in the world. She didn't make me forget about Beth, not even close, but when I woke up with Sandy's legs wrapped around me, her arms holding me tight, I wasn't complaining.

The first time I put myself inside her, Sandy and I had already been dating for a month. I felt comfortable with her. Sandy was really tight, much tighter than Beth felt to me. She wasn't cocky like Beth in bed, but sweet and vulnerable. The fact that she was tight down there—it just made me even more confident. She got a lot of pleasure from our sex—that is, after some practice for both of us. At first I came pretty fast, but over time I lasted longer and, after ten or fifteen minutes of making love to her, generally she had an orgasm. A really good one even caused her to call out "I love you!" once … even though I think we both kind of realized we weren't in love. She had a boyfriend back in Wisconsin and she knew I had another girl on my mind.

Sandy did wonders for my confidence. Once while we were lying naked as the sun rose, she said as she stroked me, "I can't believe how small it is, when it's soft, I mean. But when it's hard, it gets so big." Things like that make you feel really good if you're a college boy, especially one trying to get over a bizarre sexual encounter.

Sandy and I didn't so much break up as stop sleeping together. I almost missed her more in the summer when classes were over; I really enjoyed studying with her. We had a knack for having fun but still hitting the books just enough. When she left for Wisconsin, I got a job on campus for the summer. Why go home? I wasn't sure what was there for me.

That first work summer wasn't the greatest. There were only a handful of student employees living on campus, and the girls paired off pretty quickly—at least the ones I was interested in. I spent my time after work biking, hiking, and writing. I was starting to learn a key lesson for my particular life: turn your loneliness into a positive.

By the end of that summer, I had lost some of the confidence I had developed with Sandy. It didn't help that she didn't write me back. She didn't have an email address—many of us didn't back then—and I didn't even have a phone in my room. It also didn't help that I had a crush on a girl who had a big bodybuilder for a boyfriend. She lived in the campus apartment next to mine and, on the hot nights when our windows were open and he was in town, I could hear her moans and screams.

The next school year brought some interesting times my way. That was the year I met Vee—her name was Veronica, but everyone called her "V." If I fell in like with Sandy, I fell in love with Vee. It was almost the type of innocent high school romance you never had in college.

It was October of my sophomore year, and we were at a party. This time, instead of trying to develop a friendship, I just summoned my guts five minutes after meeting her and said, "You wanna go somewhere and make out?"

She laughed, and said "Yes." Everything flowed perfectly with Vee. She was the first to confess, "I think I might love you." And it wasn't because she was cumming, either. I remember walking home from her dorm the night she blurted it out. There was a happy buzz in my life at that time, a feeling of inevitably. *You could marry this one.*

Vee and I lasted until halfway through my junior year. I'll never know exactly what caused our breakup. It seemed like we were fighting more often. She was taking some "women's studies" courses and she seemed to get more militant about my language. She'd get riled up at things I might say, and we'd be up late arguing about stupid things like whether men should hold doors open for women at restaurants. These trivial arguments would lead to almost shouting matches. She would go back to her room and we wouldn't talk for a day or two. I would apologize, or she would. We'd try to have make-up sex, but it wasn't very inspiring. Once I tried to recapture some of our early sexual spark by throwing her down on the floor and just ravishing her, but the whole thing was off. I had trouble getting inside her for the first time. It only dawned on me later that it was because she was so dry down there, so *not turned on* by the sex we were trying to have.

The breakup isn't anything I like to think about now. This is the first I've recounted it in many years.

We were at breakfast in the school cafeteria, talking about the classes we were going to take in the spring. I choked down a bit of oatmeal, but I felt woozy as hell. Vee said something about getting her biology textbook back from me. It was a random comment but it had a creepy finality to it. Before I knew it, I was asking her, "Are you breaking up with me?"

Ten minutes later it was done, and I was carrying my tray to the dishroom, fighting off the tears. I managed to make it outside. I thought I was crying for Vee, and I'm sure I was. But maybe I was crying also for the end of my vanilla "Jason as Alpha Dog" sex life. What I do know is that all these years later, I have never really felt like THE MAN in a relationship again. From then on, the harder I tried to be the "wanna go make out?" alpha dog, the more it eluded me.

For the rest of my junior year, I had an excuse. Heartbreak. I avoiding the dating circuit, knuckled down on my major. There were plenty of things to think about besides girls. I was living on a quiet corridor that had been designated a study hall. No one had much fun there, at least not of the loud variety. There was no one to be jealous of. We would have tea in the lounge around 10 p.m., and then it was off to our rooms to hit the books. It was closer to a monastery than college.

Vee had moved to the housing unit farthest from me, so I didn't see her in the dining hall. Things went better for me when I didn't see her. I avoided getting any updates on what she was doing or who she was dating. Once in the spring, I saw her in cutoffs and a Cure t-shirt, listening to some wannabe music legend strumming his acoustic in one of the quads. I turned the other way, but not before I saw her laughing and smiling with her friends, radiating with that Vee energy that I was trying to find a way to live without.

As was my habit, I worked on campus that summer heading into my senior year. I was relieved to know that Vee was back in Montana, nowhere near the campus. It didn't bother me that I didn't date at all that summer. This time, I joined a campus construction crew and worked ten hour days, often in old campus buildings without air conditioning. I would get home, throw my sweaty clothes on the railing to my tiny loft, and crash and start all over again, working overtime on Saturdays when I could.

Chapter 5

━

IN JULY, I MADE a fateful decision. I still had my place reserved on the "quiet hall," but I was thinking for my senior year it might be more fun to be in a different dorm. It was my final year in college; I felt like I was missing out on something. The campus had a new program called "teaching advisors." You could live on the top of one of the freshman dorms, in larger apartments that used to be for professors. The idea was that an upper class student could live in the dorms and offer workshops and guidance to younger students. It wasn't quite like a Residential Advisor because there were no day-to-day responsibilities. Once a week or so you gave a workshop in the dorm and had open house hours for younger students.

The apartment spaces were awesome. The only catch is that you had to share the apartment with one other student who won the other spot in a housing lottery. Yeah, you did have to share a large bedroom, but there was also a living room, a TV room, and a huge outdoor balcony.

For roommates, you had to draw straws. I ended up getting this guy Zach as my roommate. Zach was a classic computer geek. He got a reputation his freshman year for hacking the library computer system. It was the kind of stunt a hacker did in those days before the Internet exploded. For his trouble, Zach was given a suspension but when he came back, he made amends by offering to improve the security on the system. He eventually got a job in the computer lab there. Soon he was helping on computer science classes, and he probably knew more than some of the teachers.

I figured Zach might be the perfect roommate—away from the room a lot, probably not bringing girls around too often. I'd have the bachelor pad to myself. I knew him a little bit back when he was a freshman. At that time, Zach was one of the most socially awkward guys around. I don't recall him dating anyone seriously. He wasn't bad looking, I guess. His matted black hair hung carelessly over thick-rimmed glasses. On good days, he probably looked casual and indifferent. On bad days, he was a geek stereotype. He was tall and skinny but painfully shy, especially around girls. At least as a freshman. The last couple of years, he had lived off campus and traveled in different circles.

Turned out Zach was in town that summer, working at an off-campus computer shop. When he and I met up to discuss living together, I remember thinking there was something different about him. He still had the glasses, but the hair was more of a spiky punk-rock look. He shook my hand with confidence, and his geekiness seemed to have given way to a snarly "I don't give a fuck" vibe. It was a fairly striking transition and I found myself even more curious to be his roommate; I was not opposed to making a similar transition. He seemed like he had remade himself into a whip-smart badass. It sure beat the nice guy routine I seemed to be falling into. We agreed to make a go of it in the fall.

The summer was uneventful. I ended up staying in a faculty apartment off-campus, house-sitting for most of the summer. Perhaps some would have thought it a lonely time, but not me. I wrote my first novel then. It was bad science fiction. Even as I was writing it, I knew it was bad. But I could sense something else—a discovery. When I pulled back from the outside world, I could get something done. I could change myself. *I had written a book*. I knew it wasn't good, but it was better than going to bars with my friends and hoping we wouldn't get carded, only to stand awkwardly in the corner without knowing how to approach the girls I wanted. Discovery #2: I did a lot better socializing with girls in less pressurized situations, like study groups. The study groups would return in the fall. That would be my time. My senior year.

The fall started out really well. The top floor apartment was nothing short of spectacular; you could see the mountains out of the sliding glass doors. We even had a little grill on the outdoor patio for cookouts. I know what you're thinking. How would they let college students have a top floor outdoor patio? I understand they gave those spaces back to faculty in recent years.

The apartment was a serious "girl magnet" location. The first day Zach and I got in there, we gave each other whooping high fives. We set up bamboo curtains in between our main areas, and Zach let me keep the couch on my side. Each of us had enough room for a bed, as well as huge desks made up of doors on wooden blocks. With a fridge and a row of speakers in the TV room, even a guitar and an amp, it was impressive college living. I was soon getting visits from several girls from my past, friends I had made along the way, Zach's friends as well. Everyone wanted to check out the new pad. A few bean bag chairs and a strobe light and we were ready for anything.

Even by the first weekend, you could tell it was going to be an interesting year. That part did not disappoint. On the first Friday night, after all the students arrived, my friend Lisa stopped by. It was amazing to see how much she had changed since spending her junior year in France. She was a short, sporty girl from California, and I'd always had a crush on her, or at least I was in lust with her. She had taken to hanging around with a couple of friends who were younger, Alexis and Becky, because she had to take a basic biology class that most students get out of the way early. But she screwed that up and had to take the class late in the game, and in the process met some younger students. I had no objections when she invited them over to my place. Soon the four of us were sitting in beanbag chairs and passing around expertly rolled marijuana cigarettes that Lisa had bought from the biggest druggie in our dorm. When things got late, the conversation got wilder.

Then Lisa said, "You know, I have the keys to the pool."

"What?" I asked her. Lisa had helped with outdoor first aid instruction classes in years past, so taking the keys home was no big thing.

"I've always wondered what it was like to swim in the pool after it was shut down for the night," she said.

One detail I should mention that factored heavily into my story: on the first day of school, Zach's parents sent him a computer, which arrived in huge Circuit City boxes. It was a far better model than we had in the library. As soon as he set it up, I had a feeling I would be seeing a lot more of him.

That's why he ended up at home on that Friday night when Lisa, Becky and I were plotting our pool plans. It didn't take much persuading for Zach to join us for a round of smokes, especially once he got an eyeful of those three girls. To this day, I have trouble recalling a more appealing combination. It wasn't just their natural good looks; it was the forces of their personalities. You hear all the time about girls not being comfortable in their bodies or being overly nice. Not these girls—they swore like sailors and seemed ready to take off their clothes at any opportunity, and not necessarily with sex in mind either, but simply to feel free and unconfined.

I felt a twinge of jealousy knowing that Zach was around and that I wouldn't have the three of them to myself. The night got late, but Lisa wouldn't let it go, "Hey guys, let's go for that swim!"

"But if we get busted, you could lose your job," I said, feeling a bit awkward without knowing quite why.

"I think if we wait till two a.m. we should be okay," Lisa said. "My legs are really sore from the hike today and I could use that whirlpool right about now."

To my surprise, Zach accepted. I thought for sure he'd want to stay and crank out some code.

"Cool!" Alexis and Becky said, almost in unison. It was already one a.m. Killing an hour with that crew was not hard.

I was a little nervous as we jumped over the fence outside the gym. It seemed like we were tempting fate. But soon, Lisa had the exit door open for us and we were at the indoor pool, taking our clothes off, feeling the warm blasts from the heating vents that should have been shut off by now. Along the pool walls were some neon signs commemorating past championships that were also evidently not shut off at night, so you could see better than I expected inside, though everything had a red hue. I had *almost* forgotten to be uncomfortable around these girls. Hoping to appear liberated, I wasted no time stripping off all my clothes and jumping in the pool before anyone could get a good look at me. Zach lingered, wrestling with his shirt buttons.

I heard the girls jump in and looked up to see Zach fiddling with his belt. I started to feel bad for him, thinking he was nervous. That was when it dawned on me that the girls were watching him expectantly. When Zach's pants came down, I heard a couple of gasps and then, "Wow!"

Even in the red light you could see that Zach had something big dangling between his legs. All three girls were staring avidly now.

"C'mon in, Zach!" Alexis called out. "It's not that cold … not that you have anything to worry about."

"No, I don't think shrinkage is a problem here," said Becky, and they all laughed. Zach walked toward the edge of the pool and you could see his big soft penis flopping. He didn't seem shy at all anymore. If anything, he seemed proud. I was relieved when he was finally in the water. We all started splashing around, and the sexual tension that had ratcheted up when Zach took off his clothes dissolved. Lisa and I went into the deep end of the pool to see who could swim faster. I was swimming behind her, trying not to think about how fine she was with her little brown body and toned swimmer's legs. The last thing I wanted to do was to get a hard-on right now.

When we finished our race, Lisa and I clung to the gutter and looked over to the shallower end of the pool. Alexis and Becky were standing close to Zach, no longer splashing around. I heard whispers and giggles but strained to hear more. I felt my own cock twitching. So much for the fun, innocent swim. Suddenly there was something at stake again.

"Let's give them a little privacy," Lisa said to me.

"We're going to the sauna," announced Lisa, as we got out of the water at the other end of the pool.

We walked through the locker room into the girls' sauna. It was still warm from the night before. Lisa turned up the temperature on the wall.

I made a point of looking away from her, just a glimpse of her small but fine looking breasts was enough to make me twitch again. I sure didn't want to get a hard-on in here.

We had never been naked around each other before, but we actually managed to shift the conversation to politics. Lisa's father was a politician, and I had been thinking about politics as one field I might want to enter, managing local or state campaigns. I tried hard to talk to Lisa about working on her dad's projects, as if shooting the breeze with hot nude girls was nothing new for me. I crossed my legs a bit to keep my cock from jutting up. I managed to maintain the pretense for fifteen minutes or so as the sauna heated up.

Suddenly we heard a louder noise—the unmistakable sounds of somebody getting fucked.

"Uh oh," said Lisa with a knowing smirk.

I felt self-conscious, so I tried to focus back on the subject at hand, but then we heard a louder "YES" from the poolroom. I thought it was Alexis but it could have been Becky.

Lisa cracked up again.

"YES!" again, a bit louder. Followed by a wail that was hard to understand. "Give it to me!" maybe.

"Okay, that's it," Lisa said. "I can't take it anymore." With that, she had her right hand in between her legs as she spread them out.

"Isn't that the sexiest sound?" she asked. "A woman screaming in sexual joy."

"Yeah …" I had to admit, it was really hot to hear a girl carry on like that.

"Go ahead, touch yourself," Lisa said. "Don't make me be the only dirty one here."

With some shyness, I went ahead and started stroking myself, listening to the moans from the pool room.

It felt great; my erection came to life quickly.

"That's it! Let her have it!" That was definitely Becky. Her voice had a way of cracking when she raised it.

"Becky!" Lisa and I said at the same time. That meant it was Alexis getting it on with Zach.

The noises were coming more frequently now.

"Get it, you slut! Fuck him good!" Becky was calling out.

Lisa laughed. I felt awkward hearing the word "slut" used like that, even by a girl to another girl. That was a taboo word on our campus. Lisa was working a few fingers in and out of her pussy with urgency; it was so hot watching her please herself like that, her brownish legs spreading wider.

The sounds in the pool room had moved to the level of unintelligible screaming. It was loud enough to be heard from the outside, but we were all too preoccupied to care.

"Oh dammit, I can't take it anymore!" said Lisa. Before I could say anything, she was straddling me. "I need some dick inside me!"

I was shocked by her attitude; I had never heard her talk like this.

"But Lisa, don't we need a condom?"

"It's okay," Lisa said, "I'm on the pill." I wasn't sure that it was okay, but there was no time to protest. Before I knew it, she had my dick inside her and was humping away.

"Oh yeah!" Lisa said. "Fuck me!"

I grabbed her and started working myself inside, moving her up and down. Then came the fateful moment: I found my mind wandering. *I suddenly wished I was not fucking Lisa. I wanted to be in the other room watching Alexis get it from Zach, to see what was making her scream like that. And I had wanted to fuck Lisa for years.* Then it was Beth tormenting my thoughts again, and that one crazy night with her sister. What the hell? I slipped out. Damn it. Focus! So I worked my cock back inside Lisa and grabbed her by the waist again.

"Harder!" Lisa implored. "Harder."

I did my damndest, thrusting up inside her.

We picked up the pace. She was grabbing my shoulders so hard it almost hurt as she slammed up and down. A couple of times I fell out, due to the vigorous thrusting, but I managed to put my cock back inside her without losing too much momentum. I could see the flashes of frustration on her face when we lost the rhythm. There was really no emotional connection between us to ease the moment. She was treating me like a sex object, and I wasn't sure I liked it. Lisa held onto me with her right hand around my neck, rubbing her clit like crazy with her left while I thrust up into her.

It was over fast. With Alexis screaming and Lisa's pussy squeezing up around me I couldn't help it. I tried to think about flowers and math problems and anything but the moment, but I found myself coming really hard inside her.

"Oh yeah!" Lisa called out. "That's so hot." She lifted herself off me, clearly pleased that she had made me cum so easily.

She cleaned herself up with a towel. The noises from the other room had subsided as well. As we left the sauna, I hoped things were winding down out there. I had a gym towel wrapped around my waist. Now I was more self-conscious than ever about being naked in front of these girls … and Zach.

Unfortunately for me, things hadn't exactly calmed down. Well, Alexis was calm. When we walked around the lifeguard station, the first thing we saw was Alexis, plopped down on a couple of inner tubes, totally fucked out. Lisa laughed when she saw her.

"Who looks happy?" Lisa said.

Then we looked over at Becky. She was kneeling on an exercise mat, working Zach's cock up and down with her hand while he sat on a stack of mats behind her. I was stunned by its length and thickness. I thought I heard a quick gasp from Lisa. His cock appeared to be a foot long. I later learned it was closer to nine inches, but it curved at the top, and that gave the impression of this big long snake. Becky was working his cock up and down with one hand while frantically rubbing herself between her legs with the other. It looked to me like she was just about to lose control and straddle his cock.

"Go for it Becky!" Alexis said, spreading her long legs a bit wider and spinning on the tire for a better view. Becky turned to us, noticing Lisa and me for the first time.

"God I really want to," Becky said, "but I can't. I'm not on the pill, and Zach doesn't have a damn condom!" Her wide hips were really rotating now as she dipped her fingers in and out. I had mostly seen naked women in porn so I was a bit shocked by Becky's hairy bush. I was really turned on by the way her hips moved unconsciously back and forth. She was totally in heat. I felt myself twitching, my own cock coming back to life.

"Lisa, you do it! If I can't do it, I want to see you try," said Becky.

Lisa looked surprised, but she hadn't taken her eyes off Zach's erection either. I was even more surprised that Becky would say this to Lisa right in front of me, almost as if I wasn't there.

Almost in a trance, Lisa walked closer to Zach, who had an arrogant look on his face, the farthest thing from the computer geek I had him stereotyped as. Becky put Lisa's hand on Zach's cock.

"Feel that," said Becky. "Doesn't it feel amazing?"

Lisa didn't say anything, but she did run her fingers along Zach's cock. Then she kneeled down next to Becky, wrapped both hands around Zach's penis, and started jacking him off.

"You go girl!" Becky and Alexis said, almost in unison. Becky stood over them, still working her pussy as she leaned her wide hips on the stack of mats.

I sat down in a folding chair, deeper into the shadows, trying to blend into the scenery. I couldn't believe I was getting a chance to watch something like this again after all these years, but I didn't want to be part of the story.

Lisa was just devouring Zach's cock, licking at the head while working it aggressively up and down with both hands. The girls called out their approval.

Then something happened I'll never forget. Becky kneeled behind Lisa and said, "Let me get your pussy ready." She reached around behind Lisa and starting teasing her with her fingers. Lisa moaned.

"Oh, you're already so wet!" Becky said. "Let's get you even wetter." She wrapped her body around the smaller Lisa and massaged her pussy. Becky had clearly been with a woman before.

I noticed Alexis was casually masturbating, watching the scene unfold with interest, her long white dancer's legs splayed over the inner tube. I felt a surge of disappointment I didn't get to see Zach take her.

As for me, my erection was getting stronger. I was rubbing my cock through the towel, fascinated by what I was watching, hoping they couldn't see me.

"Looks like Zach is ready!" Alexis said, and it was true—his cock was fully engorged. It seemed even thicker and longer than before. You could see it glistening in the moonlight from its adventures inside Alexis.

Zach moaned and got an impatient look on his face. He stood up, grabbed Lisa—a bit roughly I thought—and led her toward a stack of mats.

"No, wait!" Becky said. "I want to get a good look at this," and with that, she took an extra mat and put it down on the floor.

"Get on the mat!" Zach demanded, and Lisa obeyed, spreading her thin brown legs wide and putting her hand in her pussy compulsively. I was shocked. *Here was this academic, all-American girl turned wanton slut, laid out on her back, begging for cock.* Plus she was my friend and must have known I was still there, but she didn't seem to look over at me or give me a thought.

Zach kneeled over her, slapping his big wet cock on her stomach. It seemed to go up to her belly button. Her little body looked amazing thrusting around for Zach's cock. He was totally in control.

"Be careful," Lisa said. "I'm not used to such a big cock!"

"Oh you will be soon!" Alexis called out.

As Zach started to work his head inside her, I found myself hoping either that it wouldn't fit, or the size wouldn't be any big deal. *I didn't want his cock to feel different than mine inside her.*

"Oww!!!" said Lisa as he started working his head in. I wondered if Zach's head was bigger around than his cock.

Then we all heard a loud plop. That was Zach's head moving fully into Lisa's pussy.

Alexis and Becky laughed.

"Owwww," said Lisa again. Zach took his time, careful not to bludgeon her with it. He pushed it in just a little more, most of his cock still outside her. I was relieved—it seemed that Zach's cock was bringing more pain than pleasure—but then …

"Wow!" was Lisa's next comment, and both the girls laughed.

Nobody expected what happened next: Zach pulled his cock all the way out.

"Put it back in!" Lisa implored.

"Yeah, put it back!" said Becky impatiently.

"She has to beg me for it," Zach said, smiling wickedly. He looked her in the eyes. "Beg me for it."

I was glad. I could never imagine Lisa doing that.

But without any hesitation she said, "Please, Zach, give me that cock. I want to feel it so bad!" And for emphasis, she pushed her pussy hard toward him, almost spearing herself on it before he pulled out of reach again.

"Give it to me!!" Lisa yelled.

I noticed a change in Alexis. No longer casually watching, she was intensely staring now, moving her fingers in and out with more urgency. Becky too. Just like me, the girls were entranced by how Zach was conquering this do-gooder, "always in control" Alpha girl.

Zach pushed himself into Lisa again. More grunts and moans. Once his cock head was inside her, he pushed himself down on top of her and held her arms to the mat.

The next few minutes are so difficult for me to think about; it's all I can do to write about them now. Lisa was screaming bloody murder and shuddering with orgasms while Zach casually worked himself around her, not really even fucking her hard, just thrusting in and out slowly, almost in a circular motion. The intensity of her pleasure was incredible to watch. I felt both turned on and inadequate, remembering our quick and inconsequential fuck.

I couldn't see all that well from where I was sitting in my effort to be unobtrusive, but I was fascinated by the long slow strokes Zach was taking. You could see how high he was raising himself up without slipping out. After a few of those strokes, Lisa couldn't help herself and wrapped her legs around him, pulling him deeper any way she could. When that didn't get her enough depth, she grabbed his ass. Watching her be such a wanton, sex-crazed animal right in front of me was too much. I had my cock out from under the towel now and was stroking it like crazy.

But that was nothing compared to the violent sex that soon ensued. I guess Zach realized Lisa was ready and wet enough for him because he pushed into her all the way for the first time.

"Owwww!!" said Lisa, but her cry wasn't convincing as pain; it sounded more like pleasure. Zach was pounding her harder, savagely. I could see her brown body glistening with sweat in the humid pool room as she pulled him into her with abandon. That's when the crazy talk started.

"Oh I love your big cock, it feels so fucking good!" said Lisa. You could hear this loud plunging and slapping sound as Zach had his total way with her.

"Fuck yeah it feels good!" called out Alexis in encouragement. "C'mon Zach, make her pussy cum as hard as you did mine. I wanna see it! Make her lose it!" Alexis clearly enjoyed seeing Lisa so out of control. Lisa had been her student manager on a couple of work study jobs, so she must have loved the sight of her outside her bossy element.

"Okay, you little bitch, I'm gonna make that pussy cum!" said Zach.

Lisa had just had a heated argument last week with some guy in her dorm who called someone a bitch. But she seemed to love it when Zach talked to her that way.

"Oh god, you're right, I'm gonna cum again, I'm gonna cum so hard for you!" I could see Lisa's wiry legs pushing up frantically, eager for his cock. Knowing exactly what he was doing, Zach seemed to sense her orgasm. He stopped pushing, holding her hips close as she shuddered and spasmed all over his cock.

It wasn't until the next day when I realized how violent the sex between Lisa and Zach had been, when Lisa showed up at the dining commons with rashes on both her arms from bracing herself on the mats.

I was amazed I hadn't cum myself; I was so damn hard. Perhaps cumming a few minutes earlier had slowed me down this time. Alexis seemed to be cumming also, her fingers jammed up inside her and she thrashed around on the inner tube. Becky was a bit more under control, as if savoring the moment. She was starting to move her fingers in and out more aggressively, getting a rhythm going as she watched from the edge of the mats.

Zach pulled out of Lisa; you could hear his cock plop out of her with an obscene-sounding suction. All the girls laughed.

"God that sounds gross," said Becky.

"It doesn't feel gross," said Lisa.

Not wanting to be noticed, I stuck my cock back under my towel as best I could with it still hard. I suddenly wanted to go home. But I also wanted to stay, stay right here—that was the honest-to-god truth. *I wanted to stay here and watch these girls I desired and respected get broken down by Zach.*

I was about to get my wish, because Lisa wasn't done. She moved around on the mat and stuck her ass up in the air for him. "Give it to me from behind," said Lisa. "I want to see what it's like." The problem was that Lisa was now facing me. I could see her smallish tits hanging down and her eager expression. She made a point of not looking at me, but I was directly in front of her, lurking in the shadows less than ten feet away.

Zach was only too willing to comply, and as he walked around her, his big fat cock dangled way out in front of his skinny body. He had morphed from strange dude to sexual savant. And it was clear he had the experience to back it up. "Wow," said Alexis. I suppose we were all thinking it. Zach got behind Lisa and slapped his cock hard on her back. I couldn't see it from the angle I was watching, but I could hear the flesh on flesh. I could see Lisa's face in the red light, and so I saw her quick flash of pain as Zach worked his head in again. Then after that, pure, intense, riveting pleasure. Just the kind I was hoping she wouldn't feel with Zach.

She was lost in her own world as Zach worked his way in and out of her again. Then, without notice, she looked at me. Locked eyes with me. As if to say, "That's right, I'm getting fucked." I thought I saw her flash a knowing smile. It's a look I've grown more familiar with in recent years. It translates into something like, *"Go ahead, stroke your dick and watch me fuck. I knew you were a little pervert."*

I couldn't take it—watching Lisa's face light up in so much pleasure. I pulled my cock back out from under my towel again, hoping Lisa wouldn't notice, hoping she was too far gone. But Alexis noticed. Before I could say anything, she had walked over to me.

"Oh you're a dirty one, aren't you?" Alexis asked teasingly, looking down on me stroking, towering over me with her lanky bombshellness. I felt a flash of shame. I almost told her I'd already sex with Lisa but it would have sounded feeble. My erection seemed to get even harder with Alexis looking down on it, hands resting confidently on her hips. I felt the relief you feel when the jig is up. As she looked down on me, her white skin glowed in the red. She looked like a panther. She was the youngest of the three women; there was something very arrogant about her supple beauty.

Before I could say anything else, Alexis kneeled in front of me, her tits dangling. I marveled at the size of her brown areola and found myself wondering what those tits had looked like bouncing up and down a few minutes ago when she was riding Zach's cock and screaming like crazy. *What was happening to me?*

Before I could say anything, another incredibly shocking thing happened: Alexis reached out and grabbed my cock, pushing my own hand aside. It probably sounds strange for me to talk about it that way, but all I can say is, we had smoked a lot of pot and we'd all been let loose somehow, freed up by

Zach and the release of female sexual energy he had enabled.

"You like to watch?" Alexis said forcefully, in a way that compelled me to answer.

"Yes."

"My last boyfriend's roommate did too," Alexis said, stroking me. "I caught him stroking his tiny penis a couple of times after we fucked." Lisa moaned behind us while Zach took his time with her. I was hoping to hell Lisa couldn't hear this.

"His dick was small but always hard when I caught him," Alexis went on. Then, looking right up at me, she said, "Small and hard like yours."

I twitched in her hands, loving her strokes and dirty talk. This was what I had missed since seeing Beth and her sister—missed in a way I could never have admitted. I certainly never expected to experience such a turn-on again.

"Let's fuck," said Alexis. "Let's see if we can cum with them." Alexis straddled me quickly and lowered herself on my cock, her long legs draped on either side of the chair I was lurking in. I plunged in easily. "Are you in?" said Alexis.

God I hoped Lisa had not heard *that*! "Yes" I said.

"Oh okay," Alexis giggled as she worked on moving herself up and down. I looked at her face to see some sign of the ecstasy Lisa was feeling, but instead I saw concentration as she moved up and down, careful not to lift her legs too high. I slipped out on the second thrust.

"I'm out now," I said quietly, hoping Lisa wouldn't hear that either. Alexis reached down and put me back in, again sliding down all the way, working up and down.

Behind us, I could hear Lisa moaning, "Yes, yes!" It sounded like Zach was picking up the pace again. I wished I could see them, but Alexis was in my way. I got my wish. Alexis hopped off me.

"Your dick is too small!" she said, this time loud enough for everyone to hear. I heard Becky howl with laughter and even Lisa seemed to suppress a laugh before going back to fucking.

"Here," Alexis said, kneeling on an exercise mat beside me, "get a good look at this fucking!" I turned beet red. Alexis reached her hand over and casually touched my cock as she watched. I can 'fess up now: I was secretly hoping—and fearing—she would humiliate me again. Alexis seemed like she could easily have done for me what Jamie did all those years ago—tease me ruthlessly—but she seemed indifferent. She continued to stroke me absentmindedly while she watched Lisa getting fucked. Maybe she was as fascinated by Lisa's facial expressions as I was. Zach had picked up the pace while Alexis and I were messing around. He was moving pretty fast. Then he did something that really shocked me: he grabbed a handful of Lisa's black hair and pulled it back hard, getting a little rough with her. But that only seemed to make Lisa want it more.

All of a sudden I saw Lisa pushing back on Zach frantically and screaming, cumming again. I was jealous beyond belief. Zach wasn't even fucking her that hard. He looked almost disappointed she had cum so soon, but before I could process that, I realized with embarrassment and ecstasy that I was cumming too, just from the look on Lisa's face and Alexis' casual stroking. I squirted—some on myself, some on her arm and shoulder.

"Oh my god your little dick squirted on me!" Alexis yelled out. This time everybody laughed. Except me. I was mortified.

I wanted to go home so bad. I wanted out of this college, this social circle. It was no longer ecstasy, now that I had cum. I felt like a depraved loser. Lisa, meanwhile, had pulled herself off of Zach's cock with another "plop" and landed on an inner tube.

I could tell Lisa felt sorry I was caught up in this. She flashed me a look of compassion before turning away. Fortunately everyone's attention was shifted, because Becky was now stroking Zach's cock, her big ass high in the air. Of the three of them, Alexis was the classic beauty, but Becky intimidated me the most. She was always kind to me, but her wide hips and big full breasts stood between us. Since Lisa had introduced us, I had always been kind of tongue-tied around her. I had seen her turn guys down in the kindest but firmest way possible. She was a series of curves and sexual energy but refused to act sexual in my presence. Until now.

"God I want to fuck this so bad!" Becky said, shaking Zach's cock with her hand and pointing it at Lisa, who moved back, surprised. The girls laughed.

"No Becky, you can't! You're not on the pill," said Lisa, who was passionate about this kind of personal responsibility.

"Oh but my pussy wants to be fucked soooo bad," said Becky, clearly out of her mind from the dope and the sounds of sex all around her.

Lisa gave her one of her patented stares.

"Damn ... okay!" Becky said, stepping away from his swollen dick like an alcoholic pushing a beer back along the bar. "But I get to take him home so he can fuck me all morning," she added in that calm "I get what I want" tone of voice.

"I can't believe you haven't come yet, Zach!" said Alexis, as she kneeled down in front of him, latching back onto his dick with her hands.

"Yeah, let's see that big dick cum!" said Lisa, surprising me again with her frankness as she leaned into a mat and casually rubbed herself.

"Oh yes! Make that pussy-pleaser cum good!" Becky said, leaning back in and rubbing Zach's swollen balls with her hand while Alexis worked his dick. Zach fell back into a swim coach's chair, giving in to the pleasure.

Alexis wasn't messing around now. She was determined to make him cum. She stroked him vigorously while Becky worked at his balls.

Zach finally started to buckle, clearly under the power of Alexis' swaying tits. He had reached his limit. I couldn't blame him.

"Cumming ..." called out Zach as he spurted into the air. It was crazy watching him cum. I have seen a few guys cum in porn, and I have cum myself countless times, but I had not seen anything quite like this.

"Oh wow!" Alexis cried out as five or six hot blasts spurted out of Zach's cock in rapid succession. The first few shots blasted in her face before she was able to lower the spurts down to her breasts. I thought he was done. I'm not sure if it was because Becky kept rubbing his balls, but Zach kept spurting, not as quickly, but at least four or five more times. The girls all seemed taken aback; he must have cum for forty-five seconds. I had never been more jealous of another man in all my life. Looking at the sexual awe in these normally tough-to-impress girls' faces; it was suddenly too much for me.

Before I realized what was happening, I was walking off into the dark, not really caring anymore, just wanting to get away. As I was leaving I heard Alexis say, "God, I have never seen so much cum in my life … You are such a man!" Or was it Lisa saying that last part? It almost sounded like her. Ugh. If he was such a man, what was I? And why was I so turned on by it all?

I stumbled into the dark. I didn't want to go home to my dorm. I remember walking for what seemed like hours. I managed to go all the way to the twenty-four hour store, where I sucked down some beef jerky before finally returning to my room as the sun was rising.

As I opened the door, I hoped against hope that Zach was there alone, without Becky. And yeah, there's no use denying it—a part of me wanted to see the two of them together. But no one was there.

I had another lonely orgasm before going to sleep, imagining Becky having her way with Zach all night long, her big fleshy tits offered up however he wanted them. Even more intense, I imagined Zach breaking Becky down, conquering her and literally fucking that "I've got men under control" look off her face—the one I could never budge. Here I was thinking these amazing girls were looking for love—and heck, maybe they were—but in the meantime, they sure didn't mind getting their brains fucked out. *Just not by me.*

Chapter 6

⸺

I MIGHT AS WELL admit it: the next couple of months were bad. I lost all confidence. I guess I felt a little better that of the three of them, Zach ended up dating Alexis. I liked imagining the jealousy raging between the girls as he ultimately settled on one of them—no more sex games. As jealous as I was that he could score that kind of woman while still having the narrow-shouldered body of a throwback computer geek, I liked thinking of him as monogamous with Alexis, not having sex with every girl around and ruining them for other guys.

During the next couple of months, I would see them walking around campus together holding hands. Looking perfectly in love. I never found out how Zach ended up fucking Becky that night at her place but dating Alexis for the long haul. I could only imagine the drama that must have ensued.

One thing that was kind of nice: they never had sex over at our place. I walked in on them making out on the bean bag chairs a couple of times, but that was all. Part of it was surely that Alexis had her own on-campus apartment—won through the housing lottery—but as much as I hate to admit it, Zach probably had pity on me. He was almost unbearably nice to me, even leaving me extra meal tickets he didn't use at the dining commons since I was not on the full meal plan. I kind of hated him for it, but mixed in with that hate was some appreciation that he wasn't rubbing my face in his exploits. Whatever erotic adventures he was having, they weren't going down in our room.

I had secretly decided to move out at the end of the semester, hoping that a fresh start with some laid-back Deadhead friends who lived off campus would be a good change.

Unfortunately something happened in late November that screwed me up good.

Seemingly unrelated events added up. That night at the pool strained my relationship with my friend Lisa. She had thought the world of me up until that year, but then things got difficult. Recently, we discovered some controversial news about the funding of sports programs—the girls' volleyball team was on the chopping block, but none of the men's sports were. Lisa didn't want to go public yet because she felt it would violate the privacy of the conversation we'd had with a couple of faculty members. My friend Matthias, who wrote for our student paper, felt differently. I ended up siding with Matthias. Lisa was upset because she knew it would hurt her relationships with the teachers who had confided in us. Matthew ran with the story. He got the glory; I got the fallout.

From my view, it was about conviction, but Lisa saw it as a betrayal. Prior to the blowout we were planning to spend Thanksgiving together at her parents' place in New Jersey. After our dispute, that plan fell apart. She never told me not to come along, but it was understood. Lisa wasn't such close friends with Becky anymore—Zach drama, maybe?—but she was even better friends with Alexis. No doubt Lisa was venting to Alexis about her frustrations over me.

To make matters worse, I ended up hurting Alexis' feelings as well. I was a proud member of a literary journal we published each February. It was kind of a cross between a literary publication and a yearbook, with classic photos of school year hijinks. I worked my tail off to get on the editorial board.

In retrospect, I made a big mistake inviting Alexis to submit some of her poetry to the journal, an invitation that had been extended before the infamous pool night. I was trying to impress Alexis—something I had been unable to do before, during, or after pool night. I suppose the poetry invitation did make an impression; it was truly the one time I really got her attention, aside from cumming on her. (Ugh!)

Alexis submitted three poems. Her work wasn't bad— it reminded me of the poems in that book Jewel published. Which meant it wasn't great either. It was about her romantic ups and downs, each with a dramatic goth title like "Edge of Darkness" and "Waster of Souls." I thought a couple of her pieces were good enough for the publication, which was hardly a Pulitzer Prize worthy journal. To my dismay, I found out that the other two editors disagreed. They outvoted me two to one.

Fast forward to early December, when we posted a list of writers who made the cut. Alexis' name wasn't on it. I was hoping not to see her until after the long winter recess. Bad luck for me: I ran into her in the mail room. I was reading a letter from my grandmother, of all people, and looked up: blond hair and black goth eye makeup everywhere. She was staring down at me, her breasts filling out her Ramones tank top outrageously.

"Alexis, I—"

"Don't say anything!" Alexis said, clearly hurt by the rejection. "So much for Big Poetry Man on Campus." Alexis turned her back to me. God she was fine! I thought I heard some snarky laughter from a couple of bystanders. Did she make a small penis sign with her fingers? I could see out of the corner of my eye. But the laughter made me think she had done something. Ugh. I couldn't even tell her I had voted for her; we were sworn to secrecy.

Meanwhile, realizing things were getting awkward for me

on the roommate front, in mid-November, I met with the Assistant Dean of Housing about off-campus living options. As much as I liked the possibility of running into more sexual trouble with Zach, I was more concerned about my bruised ego. I couldn't take being single in the shadow of his conquests much longer.

The Assistant Dean was an attractive black woman with meticulously braided hair who always seemed to take an interest in me. She was only a couple years out of graduate school herself. I always enjoyed flirting with her at the gym, though I kept it low key since she was a staff member. Alisha wasn't afraid to lift a bit of weight on the barbells, which I found appealing. Anyhow, I made an appointment with her to request clearance to live off campus. For upperclassmen like me, this was a pretty routine process. Most off-campus housing requests for seniors were processed without much delay. As Alisha looked up my housing information, she noticed I was rooming with Zach. A funny look splashed across her face.

"Why do you want to move out?" she asked me. "Any problems with Zach?"

"No," I said a bit hesitantly, not expecting this line of inquiry.

"Are you having trouble getting work done?" Alisha asked. "During his freshman year, I know that Zach's first roommate moved out because Zach was doing too much … partying. Too many overnight guests," Alisha continued, smiling strangely. She gripped one of her braids as she talked.

Even though Alisha was just a few years older than I was, this was awkward at best. I felt uncomfortable but also horny. Alisha had an angular face and strong cheekbones. Even when she was smiling and joking, she seemed one glance away from stern disapproval. That stern side was hot to me.

"No, everything is fine," I said, trying to avoid direct eye contact. "I just want a change of pace. I don't get all my meals from the dining commons and cooking in the lounge is kind of a drag. I'd like my own place, a real kitchen."

"We don't get too many guys who want to cook. Is your cooking really that good?"

I blushed a bit. Was she questioning my masculinity? "Well, actually I am a good cook." The questions were raising my hackles, so I got up to leave. Alisha seemed amused, enjoying my reaction.

"Well, we'll let you know what we decide," she said as I headed for the door.

What I did not know is that Alisha had made the decision already. She put me on an internal list for those who had been approved for off-campus housing. As it turns out, Zach logged into the housing system a few days after that, looking to help a buddy out, and he saw my name on the list. That kind of thing was too easy for him to even qualify as hacking.

He wasn't happy when he confronted me about this right after Thanksgiving. I had barely put my suitcase down when he moved up on me and glared.

"What the fuck? When were you going to tell me?" Zach said, pounding a printout of the list on my dresser. It was the first time aside from that pool night that I had ever felt really intimidated by him—and this time he had his clothes on.

"Well, I haven't really decided yet," I told him, stretching the truth. There *was* still time to back out. "I was actually just asking Alisha about what off-campus living is like," I said, spinning the conversation on the fly. "I didn't even know I had been accepted, I thought I'd have to give my final approval. Shit, I can't believe she put my name on this list!"

"Well I hope you tell me soon," Zach said, "because if you're moving out there's no fucking way that two weeks is enough time for me to find someone I can deal with. They'll put some tight-ass stiff in here." Zach glared. Evidently roommate problems were not new to him either.

Eager to buy myself time, I told Zach I had not yet decided, told him more about my problems with the meal plan, my desire to do my own cooking. I promised to give him a heads-up before any kind of move happened.

After that, he calmed down, but things now seemed forced between us. Of course, our interactions had been stilted ever since the infamous pool night, but now Zach seemed wary I would stab him in the back. Before, it was a different kind of awkwardness, a sexual tension of sorts. Not the kind men usually have, but the kind two men have who competed for the same women and know deep down who won and who lost. Now there was downright animosity. This wasn't good.

So there you have it: I had planted seeds of doubt and resentment with the wrong, not-so-random group of people. That Friday night, I stopped by my dorm room to pick up my iPod on the way to a party. I wasn't expecting anyone to be in the room—just unplug the iPod and go. Surprise: Zach, Lisa, and Alexis were sitting down on our bean bags playing cards. The smell of marijuana blasted over me.

"Can you put the rug back?" Alexis asked, looking up at me with less irritation than usual. Maybe it was the pot. The "rug" was a wadded up towel we used to put under the door in case anyone in the room was smoking it up, bolstered with foam and duct tape. It was a surprisingly good aroma seal from the hallway. I was taken aback that all three of them were acting so friendly, though I chalked it up to "happy stoner vibe."

Hmm … three people with grudges against me, all stoned in my own dorm room. The best course of action was to grab my iPod and get the hell out. But Zach took the hand-roller they were smoking and said, "Have a rip, man!"

"Yeah, c'mon!" Alexis said, with a grin. Lisa forced a smile as well. Lisa was wearing some very short orange shorts—one of her ex-boyfriends went to Syracuse. It was too much to turn down. I sat down and bravely took a big drag. They all smiled. When I was able to hold down a big inhale without coughing, they applauded. I was a notoriously amateurish pot smoker, always coughing on the first drag.

They were playing five card draw, not my favorite poker

game, especially with the dealer picking additional wild cards. It was more of a party game than the strategy poker I fancied myself good at. But I hung in there for a few hands, trying not to win, which might piss them off even more than I already had of late. Instead of poker chips, we had peanuts in shells smuggled from the dining commons. After two rounds I managed to work my way down to my last ten peanuts. I figured with two aces I could bet the farm and lose, and get the heck out of there. But Lisa was goofing with a bluff. I thought for sure her hand would be better than mine, but when I called, she only had a king.

"Nice bluff, girl," Alexis said. "Next time try, uh, matching two cards together!" Suddenly I had about thirty peanuts again.

"Let's play a round with higher stakes," said Zach.

"Money? No way," Alexis said. "I'm out." She threw her peanuts in the middle and went to turn up the speakers. It was some kind of reggae beat, Peter Tosh maybe.

"No, not money. Strip. Strip if you lose. One piece of clothes per round."

"Okay!" Lisa said without hesitation, surprising me again. It had been a while since I saw how she acted around Zach. She abandoned her academic professionalism instantly and became a giggling high school girl.

"But no one's gonna see these!" Lisa said, propping up her small breasts under her tight blue tank top before falling backward.

"Damn I don't know about that," said Alexis. "Not if your last hand was any indication."

"I wouldn't mind a look-see," Alexis teased. Even stoned, Lisa couldn't help but blush.

Strip poker with these three was fraught with peril for me. But I also liked how Lisa's nipples were poking through her tank top. And Alexis, thinking about her statuesque body nude … And like I said, I'm a pretty good poker player, even with casual rules. Maybe I could turn the tables on them.

I sat back down.

The next hand, I ended up with a full house after trading in one card. Next time I cashed in two clubs and came back all hearts—flush. The peanuts were piling up in front of me, enough that I could even snack on a few without jeopardizing my game. But more importantly, Lisa and Alexis were down to their bras. The rule was, one significant item of clothing per loss. Only the winner kept all clothes on. So far, so good.

"I'm not sure if I still want to do this," Lisa said.

"Oh you're doing it, girl! Look at me. I'm in the same boat," Alexis said. Her breasts were a lot bigger than Lisa's and her bra was having a hard time containing them.

"Wow, your tits are out of control tonight," said Lisa. "Let's see if we can't play that bra off of you." She looked knowingly at me as I shuffled the cards. I called no wild cards, which caused groans from the group. But I wanted to play it straight, maybe even count up some cards and see if I could avoid having to reveal myself at all. I thought I noticed Alexis brush against Zach's sweatpants a couple times, as if she was fishing around, but I tried to avoid looking. I shuffled the cards with as much concentration as I could, hoping my own boner would go down a bit as well.

It's hard to describe what happened next. I've had this happen in cards before, where a bad momentum develops. It seems like you can't win. You get a bad hand, and you trade in for more bad cards. You think about bluffing, but as your hands go down in flames, you start to think your opponents can see right through you. Ordinarily, I would just ride it out, especially for peanuts. But this game wasn't just for peanuts anymore. Maybe what happened next was something a part of me wanted. I guess I'll never know.

Losing the next two rounds was the easy part. First I took off my Yankees cap. The girls didn't like that so much, arguing it wasn't a "significant piece of clothing." I begged to differ and pulled it off. Alexis did not hide her pleasure when she smoked me in the next round with four of a kind. Off came my shirt. Compared to what else I had taken off in front of them, the shirt was easy. Besides, the pot was kicking in and I was starting to talk myself into thinking these folks were my good-time pals. Zach still hadn't lost a hand since we had changed the stakes. I was relieved to win the next hand with three of a kind. Zach lost and I expected him to take off his shirt. Instead he stood up and, without saying a word, took off his sweatpants.

His big thick cock slapped to attention. I hadn't seen it in a while and had forgotten how meaty it was. He was already mostly hard. Like me, he must have been distracted by the girls in their bras.

"Commando. I knew it!" said Lisa.

Zach sat back down, ready to play another hand, but with his big cock sticking out, the whole mood in the room changed. Lisa could not stop staring.

"Wow," she said, "just wow." She was crossing and uncrossing her legs restlessly. I knew I should get out of the room right away, *just leave and go anywhere*, but I have to admit that I too, was fascinated by what was unfolding. The good cheer in the room seemed to have been replaced by a palpable tension.

Lisa didn't even attempt to hide her lust, which surprised me, given that Alexis and Zach were dating fairly seriously. I kept hoping Alexis would get pissed, but she seemed to be more curious about Lisa's reactions than upset. It dawned on me that I had critically misjudged that relationship. I decided my best hope was to win the next hand, but it was not to be. Alexis had a full house and even though she hadn't bet enough peanuts to really capitalize on it, her hand was more than enough to beat my three of a kind and put me in a tough spot. It wasn't about the peanuts anymore.

I tried to reach for my shoes as my next article of clothing to be shed, but Alexis and Lisa weren't having any.

"Oh no, that's not going to do it!" said Lisa. I wasn't used to the tone she was taking. But then our friendship had been shaky of late.

"No, let's have the pants now!" said Alexis.

A part of me was deeply afraid but, here's the thing I have to confess to you now, that I have never told anyone. *I wanted what was about to happen to happen.* Or at least a part of me did. At any rate, I felt powerless to resist their demands.

I stood up and off came the pants. I was relieved to have my boxers on. But I heard everyone laughing. Too late. I looked down to see my cock at full erection poking out of the open fly in my boxers.

"Off with those, since you don't need them," said Alexis.

"Off! Off!" chanted Lisa.

I had nowhere to go, nowhere to hide. At least during the pool incident, it had been mostly dark. And even with Beth and her sister, I had mostly been able to lurk in the shadows watching. Now I was at the center of things. And the overhead light in the room was on the highest setting. Why hadn't I killed that in favor of the lava lamp? I pulled my boxers off and sat down, compulsively grabbing the cards to shuffle the deck.

"Wait, I have to see this!" Alexis said.

"Guys, please stand up!"

Zach stood up willingly, smugly. When Alexis talked like that, you complied. I stood up as well.

She kneeled near us.

"No, move closer together." I looked over at Lisa; she seemed fascinated.

It was weird to stand next to Zach, because his skinny code geek body looked awkward next to my athletic build. I was also a bit taller.

But that's not what the girls were focusing on.

"Look at this!"

Alexis pointed to both our dicks.

"The contrast is amazing!" Alexis said.

It could not be denied. My dick had retracted a bit, perhaps wary of the attention. Zach wasn't fully hard but he was still jutting way out and bending down. He was way farther out there than I would be at full erection. Then Alexis said something I was not expecting. Something I can remember like this happened today.

"Let's measure them!"

"Lisa, do you have a ruler?"

"No."

"Then go out in the hall and see if you can find one," Alexis said.

Lisa pulled on a sweatshirt from Zach's closet and left to get a ruler.

"If we're going to measure you, we have to get you both erect," says Alexis.

"Maybe I can help with that," she said. With that, she reached back and unhooked her bra. Her breasts came tumbling out, looking even more amazing up close. I had never seen them in the light. They were full but without any sag, and her areola were as huge as ever.

Her ploy worked—at least on Zach. I could hear him groan as his cock twitched in the air.

I was getting excited also, but somehow my cock wasn't cooperating.

"Let's get you going a little bit," said Alexis. Without asking permission, she started to touch my cock with her hand, coaxing it into a hard-on.

That worked. No amount of shyness was going to stop me from getting an erection under those conditions.

"That's it … you're twitching!" Alexis said with satisfaction.

"Let's get you both all the way up!" she said with that total Alexis confidence. She started stroking each of us, one in each hand. I was hard in a matter of seconds. I kept hoping Zach was hard, but I could see Alexis working her left hand up and down his thick shaft, and he wasn't all the way there yet. I didn't want him to get any bigger!

"That's it, Zach, let's get that monster all the way up," she said. Zach's cock was so heavy it didn't look like it would rise, but with Alexis spitting on her hand and then lubing him up, he finally got to full attention. He wasn't poking straight out, but he was definitely hard enough to do some damage.

"Wow!" Alexis said, looking up at both of us. "I can barely get my hand around you," she told Zach. To me, she said, "And your entire dick is almost lost in my hand!"

They both laughed. It was true. Her hand almost completely covered my erection. Whereas with Zach, she might have been holding on for dear life, with plenty of cock to spare.

Lisa came back into the room with a wooden ruler she had obtained from someone on the hall. I found myself hoping she had not told them why. Her eyes widened.

I expected Lisa to hand the ruler to Alexis, but to my surprise she pushed Alexis aside.

"I'll handle this!" Lisa said. She started with my cock, putting the ruler up next to my erection and grabbing my cock to put it right next to the measurements.

"Four … Four point two inches," she said quietly, as if absorbing a shocking truth.

"And now …" She reached for Zach's dick, but not before looking at Alexis for permission. Alexis nodded, only too happy to be sharing this moment of triumph and humiliation.

"Eight … eight point eight inches," Lisa said. "More than twice as long!"

"Zach!" Alexis said. "I'm really disappointed in you. I've measured you at nine inches before." They all laughed.

But Lisa didn't laugh long. She had dropped the ruler and was working our cocks just as Alexis had, one in each hand. She had a puzzled look on her face.

"I think we needed a tape measure," Lisa said.

"Why?" Alexis said.

"Because we need to measure girth as well," she said. "There's obviously a girth thing going on here also."

"Yeah, Zach is WAY thicker," Alexis agreed, as she sat on the edge of Zach's bed and turned the scene over to Lisa.

"Right," Lisa said. "So let's say Zach is one hundred fifty percent thicker. If he's also one hundred percent longer, that means he's … about five times the size in volume."

"True!" said Alexis.

"But we don't have a tape measure," said Lisa, "so we can only guess."

"I have an idea!" Alexis said and left the room. I thought she might be going to the dorm office to find a tape measure —what would she have said to them in the middle of the night?—but she came back with a toilet paper roll.

"This might give us some idea," Alexis said, tossing the toilet paper roll to Lisa as it started to unravel. Lisa caught it and looked at Alexis, a little confused.

"See how it fits!" Alexis said. Realization swept over me and Lisa at the same time.

She quickly and easily pushed the toilet paper onto my cock. You couldn't really see my cock. It was hidden inside the roll.

"There it is," Lisa said.

"Yeah, you can see just the tip of his little head sticking out," said Alexis.

"Let's see how you do, Zach," Lisa said. I didn't like the admiring way she was looking up at him one bit.

She tried to slide the roll onto his head. "Damn!" she said. "I think I can get it on you, but I don't want to hurt you."

With some twisting, Lisa managed to get the toilet paper over part of the tip of Zach's cock. But that was it.

"Not gonna work," Zach said. He pulled away from Lisa and starting flopping his dick in the air. You could see the toilet roll bouncing around, delicately balanced on the tip of his cockhead. His big cock speared it. It looked absurd, and to stoned people, it looked even more absurd. Lisa and Alexis were laughing like crazy. I had a hard time laughing, but at the same time I was glad the attention was away from me. Zach seemed to be enjoying showing off how he could manipulate the toilet paper roll without actually putting his hands on his cock. I felt another flash of jealousy, seeing how he could move his cock around in the air, kind of like a third arm. The roll just fell off, unable to stay on Zach's swollen head.

But then something strange happened. As soon as Zach stopped messing around with the toilet paper, the laughing faded and the mood lapsed into lusty seriousness.

"Wow, that is one incredible cock you have there, Zach!" said Lisa, unabashedly rubbing herself under her panties.

"Oh hell yes!" said Alexis. With that, she couldn't take it anymore. She grabbed her boyfriend's cock and started sucking on it aggressively, slutting it out right in front of us.

"Zach will you please fuck me?" Alexis said, staring up at him urgently. She looked over at us apologetically. "Sorry, guys but I've been on my period and I haven't been able to have him inside me for a few days now." With that, Alexis bent over the side of the bed and stuck her gorgeous white ass up in the air for him. I hadn't even realized she had taken off her panties.

Zach took his time getting inside her, but once he was in, what followed was the most animalistic fucking I had ever witnessed … well, since the last time I had seen Zach in action. I guess the two of them had done this a lot; Zach had figured out that he could bang away at Alexis from behind without hurting her. He was pulling her hair, slapping her ass until it was red, making her crazy. He knew just what he could get away with, exactly what would turn her on.

I couldn't believe how much power he had over this goddess, or how long he could last. They must have fucked in that position for twenty minutes at brutal speeds. I turned up the music to try and drown out Alexis' wailing, but anyone walking the dormitory hall would have had a very good idea that a girl was getting a fantastic fucking inside. Every now and then, Zach pulled out and whacked his swollen wet cock on Alexis' ass; she would push like crazy, trying to get it back inside of him.

I realized Lisa was on the bed behind me, masturbating, all her clothes off, the sweatshirt discarded on the floor.

Meanwhile, Alexis playfully shoved Zach to the ground and lowered herself down, nice and slow. "Ahhh," she said in satisfaction.

Lisa seemed transfixed. Her naked pussy was wet enough to leak on my bed. Remembering the last time, and how horny Lisa had been in the pool, I began to lie on top of her, thinking I could make a bold move and get back inside her.

This time she brushed me off, almost irritated. "Not now, I'm really close to coming!" she said.

Hurt but turned on by her cruel tone, I stroked myself a bit and rotated between watching Lisa feverishly work her clit and Alexis move up and down on Zach, taking her sweet time and rotating her athletic hips all over the place.

Before long, Lisa was cumming and trembling. I had never seen a woman have masturbation orgasms like this. I thought she was going to crush her hands between her thighs.

I was ashamed to be left out but too turned on to care. I was amazed now by how high Alexis was raising her ass off Zach's cock without losing it or her rhythm. I wondered how good that must feel inside, to get all that friction and never lose contact. From the way she looked, it must have felt incredible.

"Go on," said Lisa, "you should cum too." I realized Lisa was looking at me differently, kind of cruelly. Later on I wondered if her anger over my past betrayal fueled this attitude.

"Here, let me do it," Lisa said, sounding almost disgusted.

With that, her hands wrapped around my dick. I felt a tingling sensation shoot through me and I'm not sure I've ever been harder. For this moment, all the teasing had been worth it. Between the intensity of the humiliation and the pot and Lisa's fingers working me expertly, I let myself go. Coming from a half-interested Lisa, it was almost like a mercy hand job, but I was too worked up to care.

I thought I saw Alexis smile a knowing smile, but she was gone herself, bucking up and down on Zach. She cupped her own boobs in her hands while Zach took over the thrusting; there was something so sexy about her abandon. I started cumming all over Lisa's tight grip and into the air.

"I knew that four inch dick was going to cum fast!" Lisa said. Her intentional use of my measurements stung, but how could I argue? I had cum with just a few minutes of her hand's administrations while Zach showed no signs of cumming as Alexis bucked all over him, now a half hour into their fuck session. Alexis was close to cumming again; you could see her body quickening as she fell forward onto him, wrapping her arms and putting her face down on him, her ass trembling. Watching her powerful body cum was almost enough to force me back to erection.

Then the unexpected happened. Before they were finished, Zach got a phone call. He had agreed to house-sit for his faculty advisor that weekend, and his teacher's dog Alamo had gotten out of the backyard. Alamo was likely swimming and chasing ducks in the pond down the hill—a huge no-no. He had almost killed a duck recently, and a dead duck would mean bad news for Alamo from the neighborhood association. Telling your professor their dog was put down while you were looking after them is not a conversation a college student wants to have. Zach had to leave immediately and see if he could track the dog down. Alexis seemed especially disappointed as she put her t-shirt back on. She definitely wasn't done cumming.

"Don't you at least want me to make you cum first?" she asked Zach.

"No way," Zach said. "I want to save it for later." He jammed his half-hard dick inside his jeans, struggling to close the zipper. Alexis and Lisa smiled at the comedy of his engorged dick not cooperating with his trousers. He dragged a comb through his greasy hair.

"Are you sure you don't want me to come with you?" Alexis offered.

"No way. You're too fucking stoned," said Zach. An odd thing to say since he was just as gone as she was.

"Okay, baby," Alexis said as she giggled, not bothering to deconstruct his logic. She lunged for him once more to give him a little going away crotch grab.

"I'll wait up for you," Alexis said. "And you," she added, slapping his bulge appreciatively.

But it was not to be. We went from stoned to tired pretty quickly. The most bizarre thing of all? Lisa sort of curled up around me in my bed. It was amazing feeling her smallish breasts against my back, and her curves locked into mine. I was confused as to why she would be so nice to me after being so mean before, but I wasn't going to make an issue of it. It was almost as if Lisa, after cumming, realized that lusting after a guy she couldn't have wasn't the best idea. A bird in the hand …

Alexis scowled but then hopped under her own covers.

"I'm so stoned," she said, letting the buzz take over.

I didn't try to have sex with Lisa again, or anything like that. I had learned my lesson. The feeling of her naked body wrapped around mine was thrill enough. I wanted to apologize for our falling out but it didn't seem like it really mattered tonight. She even kissed me on the cheek once or twice. Curled up against each other like this, it was easy to fall asleep.

I tried to stay awake and savor this time of being reconnected, but it wasn't happening. No one even thought to turn the lamps off. I had turned off the big overhead light and the lamp on my nightstand, which I almost knocked over in my stupor, but the lamp on Zach's side of the room was too far away for a stoned dude to bother with. I tried to persuade myself to get up and turn it off but it was too nice feeling Lisa's breasts up against my back and her arms around me. I conked out. Years later I realized all the things I learned that night were thanks to a strange mixture of uninhibited college women and good dope—not a situation you can easily simulate. I've never had another night like it.

I dreamed that I was in a large lecture hall, wearing only my boxer shorts. The people behind me were whispering and I was concentrating on not getting an erection. But the whispers drew louder, then all of a sudden laughter my cock poked out, determined to make an appearance. I awoke with a start and was shocked by what I saw.

Down on the thick carpet between our beds, Lisa's legs were spread. Zach was kneeling between them. *When had he gotten back?* He was about to insert his big, swollen cockhead inside her. He even had a condom on, which almost made me madder. They weren't just being sneaky, but were really intent on doing this right.

"Oh yeah, put it in me," Lisa whispered. "I've been wanting this for a long time."

Lisa propped herself up on her elbows so she could see Zach's cock working its way in. My first urge was to narc on them, to wake Alexis and tell her what was happening. Yes, Zach had fucked Lisa in front of Alexis, but *Zach and Alexis hadn't been dating then*.

Before I could decide what to do, I looked over at Zach's bed. Alexis was already awake, looking down at them intently. If I wasn't mistaken, she was even rubbing herself under the sheets. So much for getting Zach in trouble. She seemed as fascinated as I was.

Lisa wrapped her legs around his back.

"Harder, Zach!" she said impatiently.

"Okay, but it's gonna hurt a bit if I go too hard," Zach said, laughing as he kept just the tip of his head in Lisa and one hand on his thick shaft.

"I don't care, Zach!"

With that, he pushed his dick all the way inside her and drove his dick home all the way to the base.

"Owwww!" Lisa screamed.

Alexis sat up with a start. I did too. There would be no sleeping in on our dorm hall this morning.

I was hoping Alexis would tell him to get his dick out of Lisa, but no. All she said, was, "Zach, you're gonna wake up the whole dorm if you do this now."

"I don't fucking care!" Lisa said. "I need it. Now do it, Zach," she implored.

"Okay then," Zach said. "You asked for it."

With that, Zach started moving in and out of Lisa, slowly at first, then faster.

Compared with the last time he had been with Lisa, this was a more aggressive fucking. It was as if they knew it could only happen once, so it had to be for keeps.

Her heels were banging on his back so hard it must have hurt him, pulling him in deeper. Same thing with her hands, scratching onto his back for dear life.

I couldn't see his cock going in and out of her, only her legs spastically pulling him in deeper, but I was fascinated by Lisa's facial expressions. She was clearing cumming. So much for Sex-Ed. I had been taught that women typically needed to rub their clits during intercourse to cum. Lisa's hands were nowhere near her clit—they were up around Zach's wiry shoulders—and yet it was clear she was cumming almost continuously now.

"Oh god, Zach, oh god!"

"That's it, Zach, show her how good you give it!" Alexis called out as she worked herself under the covers, her legs spread brazenly wide and sticking out of the sheets on both sides.

"I have to slow down," Zach said, "I'm going to cum soon."

"Oh not just yet," Lisa pleaded, as Zach curbed his thrusting.

"I want to see your ass up in the air for me anyway, you little slut," Zach commanded.

No arguments. Within seconds she had pulled his cock out of her with a noisy squelch and rolled herself over. But the condom had slipped off as well.

Alexis to the rescue. She got up, nude as all get out, and did her lanky walk to her purse. "Hold on, you two!" she said. "That big penis is not going inside Lisa without a condom."

"C'mon Zach, let's go!" Lisa said.

"I can't, Lisa," Zach laughed.

Lisa looked over her shoulder, showing some irritation. That irritation turned to curiosity as Alexis pulled out a box of Magnum XLs, grabbed a fresh one, and personally rolled it over Zach's cock, shiny and beet red with Lisa's juices.

"Okay, big boy," Alexis said admiringly, as if looking at his cock for the first time, "go help her out."

That was when Zach noticed me over at my bed. I had been stroking off, very close to cumming myself. I realized I was beyond shame or wondering who was watching. It was just so erotic to see Lisa in this kind of desperate abandon after acting so indifferent in my bed, despite our affection for each other or my lust for her.

"You want to do the honors?" Zach said, looking over at me.

"What do you mean?" I asked him, surprised.

"I mean, do you want to put my cock inside her? C'mon, she's waiting for it."

Lisa surprised the fuck out of me. "Yeah, do it!" she demanded, without an ounce of concern for my feelings.

I can't really explain what happened next, but I did it. I really did. Part of me was just curious to see what Zach's cock felt like. And part of me really wanted to see the scene continue, to do my part. I could never get enough of watching a woman receive this kind of extreme pleasure, and that holds true to this day.

I got up, trying hard to pretend that nothing would ever come of this and no one would ever remember. Before I knew it, I was walking across the room, completely naked, grabbing Zach's pole and working it into Lisa. I was amazed by how thick and heavy it felt in my hands. Nothing at all like my cock. *Nothing at all.* It actually wasn't easy to get it inside her, but it was fun to have a chance to touch Lisa's pussy lips. I could see them swelling around his large cock head as it went in with a plop. I could feel for myself what a tight fit it was.

"That's good," Zach said, smiling at me in a way that was utterly intimidating. "I can take it from here," he said in an offhand way that made both the girls laugh. Before long he had worked his dick pretty well inside her. I had a really good view of her pussy lips clinging to his thickness; it was like he was turning her inside out.

"Oh Zach, that feels incredible," Lisa said. "But I need it harder!"

"Okay, you asked for it," Zach said, pulling her ass to him while snaking himself over her back.

Zach was kneeling over her now, which wasn't so great for my view of things, but it didn't matter, I could still see Lisa's face and the intensity of the sensations splashing across it. She seemed to almost be clenching her teeth as her body shook. Zach held her ass up to him expertly as Lisa squealed and trembled. That was it. I was too far gone and started squirting, this time just a few squirts as I had cum hard only a few hours prior.

I caught it mostly in my hand and went looking for a Kleenex, relieved that no one seemed to be paying any attention to me. I put some sweatpants on while I was at it, relieved to be covering myself up again. But here's the weird thing, which I did not realize till later: *I felt ashamed by the events of that evening, but at the moment, I had never felt freer.* It was like I had looked my worst fears in the eye and said, "Come and get me, motherfuckers!" And I was still standing. Not that I wanted to go through this again.

The sexing seemed to be somewhat over for now. Zach was still fucking Lisa from behind but his pace had slowed dramatically.

"I need a break," Lisa said and pulled away from him. This time, he let her shoulder go and his mostly hard dick slipped out of her with a loud squelch and even a couple of pussy-sounding farts. It was kind of gross and the girls laughed. I was taken aback by how swollen and obscene Zach's cock looked resting on Lisa's ass.

I wanted to get out of there. Badly. But there was something pulling me back. It was as if I sensed that after college, I would not be able to see something like this again, maybe ever. *And a part of me craved it.* I headed for the bathroom, finished zipping up my sweatpants, and washed my face quickly. I could hear moaning and didn't really want to miss it.

When I came out, Zach was cumming all over Lisa's back. Alexis was stroking his cock to push even more of his cum out, his condom hanging limp and well-used in her left hand. He seemed to be spurting everywhere, and Lisa's back was completely soaked.

"I think that was close to a record, Zach," Alexis said. "I'll have to make you take a break for a few hours before cumming more often."

"We're probably going to need two towels this time."

"Jason, can you get us some towels?" Alexis demanded. I obliged obediently, somehow comforted by her command of me, as if I was her servant. But as I went to the bathroom to get the towels, I tripped over some kind of breaking point with the three of them. I'm not sure what it was.

Maybe it was feeling out of my league with a guy that needed not one, but *two* towels to clean up his cum when I generally only needed a Kleenex. Maybe it was realizing that the relationships between us were fragile as all hell, and I was the weakest link. As the therapists would say, I didn't feel safe. I handed Alexis the towels, grabbed the keys from my dresser, shut the door with some decisiveness, and was gone.

I made a point of staying out for hours, hoping they would be gone when I got back. I ended up having breakfast in town, and I spent two hours in a used bookstore, the kind you almost never see anymore where there is always another nook to explore and some dusty hardcover that you fancy might have the keys to your life somewhere in its yellowed pages.

I got back to my dorm room around lunchtime. Unfortunately, one final indignity awaited me. Taped on the door was a photo of our two erect cocks. *I couldn't even remember a camera!* Was there a camera? I guess when you're stoned, certain details escape you. In the back of my mind a repressed image of Lisa holding a Polaroid camera up close to our cocks came rushing back to me. And Zach did have a Polaroid camera. We used it once to take a picture of a friend of ours who had passed out in our room. We courteously wrote the word "SHIT" on his forehead before taking the picture. And now … Shit!

You couldn't see the faces in the camera—that would have been enough to get them kicked out of school, or at least out of the dorms. But the size difference between the two dicks was incredible, if anything, even worse than it had been in real life. You could barely see mine sticking out; meanwhile Zach's thick dick took up the whole frame, almost attacking the camera. You could see his silver wristwatch easily held around his cock, jutting into the frame. *Had they put a wristwatch around his cock?* I looked around before ripping the picture off the door. There was a voicemail on my machine from Alisha.

"Hi Jason. I stopped by to see you earlier, to talk with you about your housing request. Come by my office to … discuss."

I found myself wondering … Did she know? *Had she seen the picture?* In a way it made me excited. I made my way down to her office right away.

Alisha looked at me in a very curious way when I sat down.

"So, I didn't think we'd be able to find you a spot," she said, going for the drama even though she had already decided to move me. "But … I realize you do need to make this move, don't you?"

She seemed to be challenging me to admit that I had a serious roommate problem.

"Yes, I do."

"What I did," Alisha said, "is open up another place in a four bedroom house. There's a spot in the basement that's pretty nice, but has not been fire approved. We were going to wait until the fall, but I've called the fire marshal and I *think* we should be able to get his approval."

"Okay."

"It's a good house, two guys, two girls … quiet, seniors. A cat. Never heard anything *crazy* going on there." Alisha seemed to look up with the emphasis on the word *crazy*. It had occurred to me while she was talking that if she had fucked Zach she would likely know about his silver watch, in which case, she would probably know exactly who was in that picture with him. But surely she hadn't fucked Zach … surely?

"Sorry we couldn't get you in with the Deadheads," Alisha said. "I tried, but they have a very popular house."

"That's okay," I said shyly, feeling that mixture of shame and excitement I've come to know so well.

"And for the record," Alisha said, "you should never let anyone intimidate you. I'm letting you move so you can get into a better living situation. But you should never let anyone feel they've gotten the best of you."

I wasn't sure where she was going with this, but I really wanted her to continue.

"We can't change how we came into the world, but that doesn't mean you settle for less," Alisha said. "You keep fighting."

Alisha looked direct into my eyes. I knew then she knew exactly what we were talking about. *She had definitely seen the photograph. And she knew who was who.*

Then there was a flicker of a smile. "Someone has a … serious advantage over you in one area, you gotta beat them in another. Got it?"

I started to flush. Wow, she was just about to come out and say it. But we were in her office. Her assistant was in the next room with an open door. The moment passed.

"If you have any … problems, you come talk to me, okay?" She gave me a big hug.

I have thought about that meeting with Alisha many times in the years since. I know that she really cared for me and could tell I was in over my head in that situation. She got me out of there and into a better place. Maybe she realized I was turned on, and maybe she was too. But she realized I needed something different. I was too young to absorb that assault on my ego without losing heart.

Chapter 7

—

Tʜᴇ ꜰᴏʟᴋs I ʟɪᴠᴇᴅ with in that new house became some of my best friends, not just in college, but in life. I owe Alisha a debt for that. It was as if she sensed what I needed. She wasn't out to tease me or humiliate me. She wanted me to go out and claim my life. I think she realized I was too young and fragile for the full truth of certain things.

But in the back of my mind I have been haunted by other things she said as well. About having a serious advantage in one area. I always wondered where that conversational road would have led. You may find this hard to believe, but in the collection of erotic encounters I've had, nothing turns me on more in retrospect than this one, which was not erotic at all, except for the secrets reflected in Alisha's eyes and the use of the word "serious." I loved that she wasn't giving me the usual politically correct "size doesn't matter" BS and admitting that Zach's advantage over me was not just an advantage, but a serious one. Wow! Of course in my fantasies, she says "huge" instead of serious.

And of course if the fantasy goes further … she closes the door to her office, asking me to show her my cock, to see if it is as small as it is in the picture. She jacks me off while telling me about how Zach is so big and so good in bed that she had to have him more than once, despite the professional risk. All the while remaining completely clothed in her professional attire, her white blouse and her conservative wool skirt, as she talks with me about what it will be like growing into adulthood with my size. It's such a sexy scene because in my mind, she is both supportive *and* honest. Something I did not find for a long time.

As for Alisha and Zach, you may think I am just assuming he fucked every girl on campus, but there was a very persistent rumor that he had fucked Alisha a number of times. I heard it from a couple of people, and years later Lisa would swear Alexis told me the same thing. At any rate it doesn't matter now, but it does fuel that particular fantasy knowing it might have come close to reality.

So I entered a different time in my youth, where I tried to make something of my life and worry less about girls. It was a time of hitting the school books and hanging out with supportive friends. I finally realized that who I surrounded myself with mattered. And what I directed my energy toward mattered too. I could ether feel sorry for myself, or I could start kicking ass and make myself a man.

I decided to become a teacher, and I worked hard at it. I did internships at local schools, got involved in community teaching projects, and figured out what classes I would need to take before graduating to get state certified. After a long day, instead of coming home to some guy having sex with a girl I craved, I would come home to a Scrabble game, or sometimes even Magic: the Gathering. And my life felt right.

I learned something very interesting about women along the way. I found out that when I stopped chasing them around and focused on accomplishing good things, they were drawn to me instead. This revelation didn't rid me of the performance anxiety I sometimes felt in the bedroom, but it did rid me of my "dating anxiety."

"Do good shit, make a name for yourself and the girls will come to you," was how my friend and housemate Greg put it to me during one of our great late-night talks. He was right, and it was working.

As for the bedroom, I'd be lying if I said I had a ton of sex the next few years, but I did okay. I focused on eating pussy. Girls at my college were really into oral sex, maybe because their high school boyfriends were hopeless at it. It seemed like something I could master. I even went online and read up on techniques. I figured out exactly when to work directly on the clit with my tongue and when to pull back and work it indirectly when the clit became too sensitive. I got pretty darn good at it, maybe even got a bit of a positive reputation. I realized how much women liked to feel like you want to devour them down there. Passion and technique weren't such a bad combination.

The year went by quickly: graduating from college was a triumph for me. I even spoke as the class valedictorian. I said some idealistic things about us changing the world I no longer truly believe—turns out the world is a lot tougher to change than I realized then. But the words rang true at the time and my classmates liked that I threw down the word "bullshit" not once, but twice, much to the consternation of our school administrators.

After the speech there were high fives and an impromptu road trip all the way out to the Grand Canyon. I managed to squander a couple of months in the glorious style of youth before my final New Hampshire teacher certification course kicked in. It was crazy to think I'd soon be teaching writing and literature to junior high school students, but there wasn't any graduate school requirements beyond the state certification. I was in.

Chapter 8

—

A S YOU CAN IMAGINE, my first year in the classroom was tough. The toughest part, however, was outside the classroom.

I thought it would be cool to have my own place for the first time and live in a small town off the grid. I moved west into rural life and fell into a social hole. The rental prices were cheap and I could live like a king even on teachers' wages out there, but it was no longer easy to meet girls.

I began to drive into the city on weekends to go "clubbing," and there my old dating anxieties kicked in hard. The club life was maybe my worst self-esteem decision ever. Clubs were great for groups of guys; cocky sexual predators seemed to rule the day. I would try to flirt with girls at the bar, but it felt forced. They would let me buy them drinks sometimes, but then I'd catch them in a slow grind with big beefy guys.

The whole thing tore away at me. I was once again confused about my sexual place in the world. I seemed to have a soft spot for the kinds of über-confident women who wouldn't give me the time of day. A couple of my fellow teachers seemed to like me, but they were bland. Some of the hot-tongued women at the club just drove me crazy. One of them, Angela, took a liking to me after I picked up her bar tab and got her and a friend into a cab when they were drunk. I even called her the next day to remind her where she had parked her car.

Things changed between Angela and me after a couple of bump-and-grind sessions on the dance floor. The sexual energy between us faded and it did not even occur to me to think she was "sizing me up" by grinding her ass against me. I was terrified of the modern-woman-as-sexual-consumer, and perhaps with good reason. But I did know that once the sexual chemistry changed, for whatever reason, I was impotent to rekindle it.

Several years went by. I loved the classroom but started to despair for myself outside of it. I finally admitted that clubbing was a bad way to go. Besides, I was staying up way too late on the weekends and when you're a teacher, dragging ass on Monday is the worst. You can't just fake it in front of unruly kids and suck down coffee like you can with an office job. I was done with the clubs. I was never going to be a player, even if my dance moves weren't bad. There was a freedom to dancing your heart out by yourself on the floor, and I even got some admiring stares, but in today's clubs, it's about the bump-and-grind.

Chapter 9

WHEN YOU THINK BACK to turning points in your life, how many did you see coming? At the time I met Kristen, I was twenty-six. Perhaps young by relationship standards, I felt like I had grown up a lot. Teaching had a lot to do with it - a few years of high school teaching had imposed some discipline on my schedule. Partying into the night and taking roll-call at the crack of dawn don't mix.

I had been out of the club scene for about a year - not that the club scene in Savannah, Georgia was anything too crazy. Savannah's music cafes were more my style, and I could hit those early. I even tried my hand at a few open mikes with my trusty acoustic and not-so-trusty vocal work. My dating life still wasn't great, but it had improved after leaving the clubs in favor of volunteering for local projects, taking community college classes, and so on. I was pretty busy with work anyhow... or so I told myself.

Once again it was so much easier to meet women in those informal settings. I had starting dating casually again, even had a couple of short relationships with women I met during that time. I wouldn't say that the sex was mind-blowing, but

I blamed that partially on my own lack of attraction to the women I was dating. I hadn't found the right girl. I was forcing myself to keep an open mind, maybe to a fault. That was about to change.

At the time I met Kristen, summer was ending and so were my summer music classes. Teaching was still going well, if you accept "intense" as the definition of "well." I did at the time. I wasn't ready to call teaching my career, but I liked the summers off and the curve balls of the classroom. I was still in that youthful idealism phase where teaching in public schools for questionable pay had an allure to it. And it wasn't just being a hero. Some of the kinds I worked with really were at a crossroads between dropping out and finding a voice or a passion or some kind of way into college. That feeling of being at a fateful crossroads - it reminded me of so many of my friends. On good days, it seemed like I could maybe make a difference. The bad days were, well, enough to keep my mind open to occupational alternatives.

I thought high school students might disrespect me due to my youth, but they seemed to like the fact that I listened to their music and got most of their jokes. Plus when it came to literature and writing classes, I knew my shit. Or at least far more than they did. But there wasn't a lot to offer me socially on the job, aside from some crusty lessons-in-life from balding teachers warning me of the perils of the profession in a teacher's lounge with busted sofas. I needed to something else. I thought maybe massage would be a good skill to add to my bedroom repertoire, so that fall I signed up for a massage class. With the school day almost ending by 5 p.m., an evening class would fit right into my schedule. And I won't lie; a big part of it was the flyer.

The girl in the flyer, Kristen, was faded from the photocopy but even with the poor quality photo on dark red paper, her natural beauty leapt off the page. I could see that utter confidence I am a sucker for, but also something else: her eyes.

There was a magical combination of wickedness and kindness. She didn't look like a beauty queen but some kind of earth mother creation born out of sun, sand, and sculpted by the elements.

Even though Kristen was older than me, I felt a connection to her from the get-go. I think she felt it too. The first time she handed me a mat for our first class, there was something. And her eyes … yes, the flyer had not let me down.

It's always great when a friendship naturally flows. So it was with Kristen. I think it was only the second class where a bunch of us were standing around, drinking water from the cooler when Kristen suggested we all go out for coffee. Two hours later, the five of us were down to two. I could sense that Kristen had a boyfriend, and she had to be a good five years older than me besides—eight years older, as it turns out.

It was the way we could talk about things. Coffee became a weekly ritual, with her and I lingering on after the rest of the group dispersed. It was maybe the third coffee when she told me about her sister dying of breast cancer two years earlier. In turn I told her about a friend of mine who had killed himself his first year in college. It wasn't like we were therapy buddies, though. Just that we trusted each other from the start. We could just as easily dissolve into bouts of laughter, as she did when she learned I had memorized the names of all the Duran Duran band members. Or when I found out she actually liked watching *Doctor Who*.

The fourth week of the coffee socials, she surprised me.

"Let's get a real drink tonight!"

With her I was always up for anything, so when the coffee pals left, it was the two of us walking to a smoky neighborhood bar on a weeknight. There was nothing sexier than watching her smoke a cigarette on the bar's fenced-in patio. Something about a yoga and massage expert taking an unapologetic drag … it worked. The hard part was pretending to be just her friend when I wanted so much more. But I could tell that hitting on her would just put me in a category with so many other guys. Her body was just unfair. If you watch Jennifer Garner in *Daredevil* you get some idea of what I was dealing with. Muscular but still feminine, brave and strong but still flirty. Kristen could be intimidating … wheat grass and vodka shots with us. Kristen could make people get along so easily, trick them into drinking the most bizarre concoctions just to be a part of her world. Then we were alone again, sitting at the darkened end of the bar as the bartender stocked glasses on the other.

"So … do you have a girlfriend?"

I shouldn't have been surprised by the question.

"No…" I said. I meant to say, "Is that an invitation?" but I chickened out. Dammit I had lost confidence again.

"Can I ask … why not?"

I hesitated.

"I mean, you're a really fun guy, you're cute…"

Cute wasn't totally what I was looking for, but …

"You have a good job, you give a shit about the world … did I say you have a good job?"

We had just been talking about her history dating guys without jobs or careers to speak of, and how awkward it gets when a massage therapist has to pick up the bill. Thus her "you have a good job" joke.

"I have trouble meeting girls outside of school," I said, grasping at straws. "That's really why I took this class."

"Well, I'm going to introduce you to some of my friends if you're not careful," Kristen said.

And she did. Not right away, but over time, at parties, at concerts. Sometimes she would even show up with a guy, but I noticed with some relief it was not always the same one. I guess that turned me on a bit also, how free she seemed to feel to be with one person or another. No one had it over on her. I started trying to work up the nerve to ask her out. If she was going to show up with different guys, maybe a younger guy wasn't out of the question. I had been single for a while again, and was kind of lost. I felt like she could rope me in, teach me some things, maybe put me on a good track again. I was a little scared by the longing I felt around her and her mysterious elusiveness. I guess I was concerned I wouldn't be able to "make her mine," but maybe that was the point. Maybe what mattered was that I could make her feel good, the way she made me feel around her.

But before I could ask her out, circumstances intervened. Kristen decided to open her own massage business with a few of her colleagues. Her current boss was a bit of a tool, and I had been encouraging her to strike out on her own. Without thinking, I volunteered to be one of her first clients.

"Really? That would be awesome! And we could work on your back." I had hurt my back playing soccer, and she had already shown me some exercises I could do on my own to help stretch and loosen it. So it was arranged.

I should have realized that paying Kristen as a massage client would change things between us. I liked that I had some money to spend on a girl, so maybe I got carried away thinking I could make an impression on her by investing in her endeavor. Yeah, I was limited to a teacher's salary and couldn't exactly take Kristen island hopping, but I was making way more money than I had in college, and I was thrifty. I could afford to spend on a girl.

The first time we actually had a formal massage appointment, as opposed to her just showing me stretching exercises, Kristen's office air conditioner was down. It was unseasonably hot that summer, and a massage without air condition wasn't going to work. Kristen called me and asked if I would do the appointment at her place, where she also had a table.

Two hours later, I was there. I was a little taken aback by her outfit. She was wearing a short white skirt and an expertly beat up pink t-shirt that clung to her breasts, which were anything but small. I felt a twitch, then relief, that I was wearing tight underwear, so I wouldn't get a boner on the table.

She showed me into the massage room, which was right next to her bedroom. Just looking into Kristen's bedroom and imagining what she must get up to in there was pretty overwhelming.

"I'll leave you to get ready," she said. She lit some incense and put Native American flute music on.

I got up on the table, kicked off my shoes and shirt, and waited for her knock.

When she came in, she looked surprised.

"Um, you're not quite ready yet."

"I'm not?"

"Yeah, you see, the towel here … that's to rest on your midsection … underneath that … well, you don't wear anything."

"You don't?" I said.

"No. I thought you said you'd had a massage before," she said in that über-confident way of hers—that alluring combination of warmth and teasing.

"Yeah, I have. Shiatsu with Alexandria."

"Oh, okay … Well, this isn't Shiatsu." Kristen smiled. "For this kind of massage, you take all your clothes off. But don't worry, I won't look."

Kristen went out in the hall. I nervously got my clothes off and lay down on my stomach. I made a point of covering my mid-section with the towel. I wasn't opposed to being naked around Kristen, but not when I was basically on her turf like this.

She made no further mention of it and started to work her way up both my legs, starting with the toes and the feet. She spent quite a bit of time on the feet, which was good because it let me think about other things. But when she started kneading my thighs, I couldn't help it. Those long, sure-gripped fingers … I was having trouble not getting excited.

"Roll over for me, Jason," Kristen said. Or commanded.

I dreaded rolling over, but there was nothing I could do now. I twisted onto my side, and then my back, trying to will my erection down. But it was hard to do, watching her breasts peek out from that tight t-shirt and her strong legs outlined by her skirt, in all their yogafied magnificence. It was too much.

Kristen seemed to quell a smile when I turned over, my dick making a tent out of the towel, but she didn't reveal much. Instead, she returned to kneading my feet, working on my toes, tugging each one till it popped. *That's it, stay down near the toes*, I thought. *Or work on my neck."*

No such luck. She started working her way up my right calf again; then she was past my knee, rubbing and pressing up to my upper thigh. Damn that felt good. I couldn't remember ever being so hard. I was embarrassed about it, but I was well past the point of being able to do anything.

"This isn't going to work," Kristen said. "You're just too tense right now. Let's deal with that. I think I know what your dating problem is, or at least part of it."

With that, she reached her hand under the towel and started stroking me. I had never felt this kind of sensation from someone else's hand. She just drove me wild. My cock twitched and strained. Then without asking my permission, she tossed the towel onto the floor and took a close look.

"Yeah, I thought so," she sighed as she stroked.

"What is it?" I asked, scared and excited about where this conversation was headed.

"Jason, you have a little dick. I'm really sorry to say it, but it really is so true."

It had been a long time since someone had talked to me that way. *What was scary was how much I had missed it.* She stroked while she was talking, looking at me in a kind way, but also a forceful one. I thought maybe she would start laughing but she settled for a hint of a smile.

"This would explain your shyness in asking girls like me out."

"But does size really matter?" I asked her as she worked her hand on my cock, inspecting it more closely now.

"Oh yeah," she said. "In more ways than you can imagine. Most girls don't have the guts to be honest about it. I'm not one of those girls who keep quiet about what she needs, as I think you know by now."

"What … ways?" I asked, scared to hear the truth I had sensed for so long. And yet I wanted to know. No, I craved the truth. *Not just intellectually, but sexually*. I watched her arm flexing lightly as she casually stroked me. I was already close to cumming. I had to dial that back a notch.

"Well, for starters, I wouldn't be able to feel you inside me," she said matter-of-factly. It was like she could sense that I wanted the truth. The problem was, I couldn't tell if she respected me for asking for it, or if she felt sorry for me. Maybe both. "I fucked a cock as small as yours once. He tried real hard, but he couldn't do anything for me. I had to put his mouth up on me instead. You'd slip out a lot, too," she added. "I'd have to concentrate just to keep you inside. That's not a problem with a nice big cock." She stared at me to let the truth sink in, continuing to stroke me with her right hand.

I couldn't recall being harder in my entire life. I willed myself not to cum, but it was too late. Looking at how ruthlessly she had eliminated me as a sexual contender, and how directly, imagining her wailing and slamming on a big cock, losing control, *getting fucked by someone who was not intimidated by her sexually like I was* … It was all too much for me.

"Oh my god," I said as I squirted, feeling my body quiver with ejaculations.

She lunged for the towel, but she hadn't expected me to cum so fast either, so some of my cum landed on her pink shirt.

"Yeah, not a big surprise there," she said, almost talking to herself as she wiped the cum off her arm and shirt before wiping it off my belly. She laughed a little bit, but it didn't really hurt my feelings. She wasn't a mean person. From my experience, mean would have meant leading me on. Mean would have been cheating on me or breaking up with me for no reason. It was impossible to be mad at her for shooting straight. *Not to mention making me cum and not ignoring me sexually like so many beautiful women had done.*

"Well, at least you're relaxed now," she said. It was true.

That orgasm had really cleared my body out; I was floppy loose all over. She put a new towel back over my midsection and went to work kneading my shoulders and neck before finally flipping me over again and working on my sore back. The talking stopped. I actually dozed off for a while, feeling more relaxed now that the scene was over and my towel covered me up again.

When the session was over, Kristen woke me, leaving the room so I could get dressed. As I zipped up, I felt sad. Here I had been thinking I might make love to her someday.

Kristen had a glass of water ready for me in the living room. She patted the couch for me to sit and drink. It felt strange to cut her a check for what had just happened. Or maybe it was illegal.

"Are you feeling … discouraged?" she asked.

I wanted to deny it, but she asked me so directly, looking right into my eyes. There was really no way I could.

"Yes," I confessed.

"Oh, don't be," she said. "First of all, not all girls care about … well, size. I guess most of us do," she smiled to herself, perhaps a little too wickedly, "but you only need to find one."

"I've been looking," I said.

"Well, it may take some persistence," Kristen said. Again I thought she might laugh but she just smiled a bit, as if thinking about some of her friends and what they would say if they knew my real size. "Hey, I have an idea, if you're up for it. Why don't you come back for a while, see me here every week? We can work on your back—it needs some more fine tuning— but I can also help you with your … confidence. We'll do the appointments here … at my place."

"My confidence?" I asked her.

"Yeah. You said you were feeling discouraged. I think I can help you through that."

What the heck did she mean by that? And where would this lead?

Of course I immediately agreed. I was terrified but also drawn to her piercing grasp of my insecurities. I wanted to see where it would go. How could she make me more confident? That I would have to see to believe. But the fact was, I was in a sexual dry spell. I didn't have other options at the moment, and that was the best cum I had experienced in months.

The next time I came to see Kristen, a part of me was hoping she would be dressed professionally. Again I was disappointed. She seemed to have an endless collection of faded t-shirts that clung to her breasts just a bit too much. This time, she was wearing jeans that hugged her hips unfairly. God, how I wanted her!

She led me into the massage room.

"This time, no towel," Kristen said. "Just get naked." She stood with her arms crossed, waiting for me to strip.

I looked at her, uncertain.

"Look, I already saw you last week," she said. "Part of your job here is to get comfortable being naked around me, not shy at all, okay?"

I nodded. That's when I realized I was excited. She was pretty much a guaranteed adventure for me, no matter what happened. I was excited as I took off my clothes. My erection popped right out and Kristen couldn't help but crack up. I couldn't tell if she was laughing at my size or just that I was already hard just being around her.

When I lay down on the table, my erection was still mostly up. She laughed. "That's okay. It's nothing to be embarrassed about." She came up to the table and started working a bit on my feet, as if she handled men with erections all the time.

"So here's the plan," she said. "We're going to do this kind of like the military."

"We're going to break you down and build you back up. When we're done, you'll be ready to go out there and break hearts."

"Break me down? I feel broken enough already," I said.

"Yeah," she said, "you're discouraged, but you're still thinking about your chances with girls the wrong way, and it's not going to work."

"So what is going to work?"

"Acceptance," she said. "We're going to start with acceptance." By this time, she was working her way up my legs again. Her firm hands felt amazing. You could always sense that she was holding back on the amount of pressure she was exerting. But that she could inflict more at any point.

"Acceptance of what?" I asked.

"Small penis acceptance."

My cock twitched.

"That's the first step," Kristen said. "You need to totally accept who you are. It may be hard at first"—she had a trace of a wicked smile again—"but eventually you'll embrace your identity completely, with its advantages … and limitations." As she spoke, she was staring at my cock. God, her honesty was refreshing. So firm, but yet not cruel.

"And," she added, "I'll teach you how to use all of it … to get … what you want …"—she rubbed and squeezed my calf muscles as she talked, loosening me up as she went—"from girls!" she added finally, somewhat unnecessarily.

That sounded pretty good, if it was possible. But I was more afraid of what might be coming next.

"Okay."

"So would you agree that you are building up to a big orgasm?" Kristen asked.

"Yes," I had to agree, hoping, praying—anything—that she would touch me again.

"Good," she said.

Then she reached into her pocket, got out a condom and opened it.

"This is one of my boyfriend's condoms," she said. "Or, more accurately, this is the condom from a guy I recently fucked." She opened it out to its full size. "As you can see, this condom is specifically made for large penises." Kristen stretched it out as she talked. It seemed to be nine or ten inches long. "I can't tell you how many times I have slid this extra large size condom on a big cock, usually in a hurry, with my pussy all tingly and itchy. Now I'm going to put this condom on you."

She slid the base of the condom on and quickly rolled it up my shaft. "Yeah, just what I thought," she said.

"What?"

"You are very loose in here, can you feel it?" she asked me.

"Yeah," I said. She had to bunch her hand around the condom to get a grip on me inside.

"But you're really hard, aren't you?" she teased me forcefully.

"Yeah."

"That's it," she said, stroking me with her right hand through the condom. "Let's get you even harder if we can!"

I couldn't imagine being any harder, but seeing her muscular arm flexing and her eyes teasing me, I felt like I was going to burst. But I wasn't ready to cum yet. Or at least I didn't want to be.

"Okay, I don't think you're going to get any harder, so let's see where we're at." With that, she placed her right hand at the base of my cock and held the condom in place. With her left hand, she pulled out the end of the condom, stretching it out into the air.

"Take a look at that," Kristen said. "There's more empty space above your penis than there is you inside it. You're swimming inside there! And look at the thickness." She showed me, pulling easily at the base of the condom. "There's no way you can realistically wear this condom. We'd have to attach it with a rubber band." She actually laughed out loud at that, having felt my cock twitch and jerk involuntarily.

"Let's try something." She pulled at the tip of the condom, which slipped off my cock with no resistance.

"Wow," Kristen said, "let's just hope you are never with a girl who only has this size condom. Actually that's a good lesson for you. You should always carry around a snugger condom. Okay, I think we're getting close to the end of today's lesson. I know this isn't easy for you, so I want you to get some enjoyment out of this."

With that, she moved to the right side of the table and put my hand on her right breast, covered only by her thin shirt— no bra.

"Do you like how that feels?" she asked.

I was amazed by how firm and large her breasts felt to my touch; I had never felt a pair that large before. They dangled down naturally and she was clearly fine with that. I could see her nipples protruding sharply.

"Here, let me help you with that," she said, and she pulled off her shirt without hesitation. Suddenly her big full breasts were swaying, and she had my hand on top of them.

"Does that feel good?" she asked.

"Oh yeah," I said. My cock was so hard it was painful, and she wasn't even touching me at the moment.

"Okay, so we're going to play a game to test your endurance. Small guys like you are always shooting off too quickly. I think it's because you don't have much sexual experience. You need to learn how to last longer, to show some ability to get into a rhythm. I'm going to stroke you, but not too fast, and I want you to stroke my breasts as well and try to hold off from cumming as long as you can, okay?"

"Okay," I said, uncertain of my staying power.

"Mmm …" she said. With her left hand, Kristen guided my hand to her breast and showed me how she liked it touched— not too roughly, but more firmly than I would have thought.

She showed me how and when she liked her nipples pinched—again, harder than I thought, but not when they were fully aroused.

With her right hand, she continued to stroke me with the condom on while instructing me. I was imminent.

"You like holding those big tits."

"Oh yeah …"

"You're pretty lucky. It's been a long time since I let a guy with a dick as tiny as yours see me naked. I let my lovers put their big cocks in between my tits all the time. The guy who donated his condom for us … I lick the head of his dick from between my tits. Maybe we should try that sometime."

The casual stroking continued.

"You'd get lost in between these tits," she said, "just like you'd get lost inside my pussy." No laughing this time, just a firm look. "You do realize pussies like to be filled up, right?"

"Yeah," I said.

"Yeah, we really do like to be stretched. You should see how I act around a guy who can really fuck me."

Her grip was getting firmer around the condom.

"The first time I met Lee," she said, "our condom owner, "I felt a shock wave go up from my pussy, up through my body and out my nipples. I just knew what he could do to me."

"How did you know?" I asked her.

"It was the way he looked at me," she said. "It was as if he could see my pussy cumming all over his cock, whether or not I liked him. Like it was already decided he would one day get inside me and make me cum."

She was stroking; I was caressing her breasts, squeezing her nipples just like she showed me.

"Two days later, I was flat on my back for him. His big cock was pounding into me, and my pussy was cumming all over it. I had a serious boyfriend at the time too, but I couldn't help myself. I was lucky he had a big size condom with him, I wouldn't have been able to stop myself from fucking him either way. He probably could have forced me out of my relationship and into his bed permanently if he had wanted." Stroking me a bit more intensely, she added, "But you're not like that."

"I'm not?" I asked, wanting but dreading her answer.

"The first time you looked at me, I could tell how smart you were, how kind, how wise. But I could also tell I'd be able to conquer you easily. That I could have you whenever I wanted. And I was right, wasn't I?" Another teasing smile.

"Yes." I had to admit it.

"Deep down you're not sure…" she said.

"Sure?" I asked.

"Not sure if you could really please me."

I was quiet.

"Are you?"

"No," I admitted.

"It's good you feel that way," she said. "Fucking my brains out … That's not your job. That's not a job your little dick could handle now is it? Not that you will ever find out," she added firmly, locking eyes with me.

With that last bit of brazen sexual truth I couldn't take it anymore. I started bucking and cumming into the condom.

"Uh-oh, you lost control!" she said, laughing with satisfaction.

"Oh wow!" I said, spurting and spurting inside the condom. I felt like I came a ton. The orgasms welled up from some deep place only she had access to.

"That's it," she said happily. "Empty that little dick for me." She gripped it with her left hand while stroking my balls with her right. It felt amazing, but I was cleaned out, just a couple of drips left.

"See, that's really hot. You really turn me on when you do what you're told," she said. "Wanna see?"

"Okay," I said.

She walked closer to my face, slid the jeans off her hips and her nude body came into focus. She had that devastating mix of athletic and curvy. If she had any insecurities about her body, she was perfectly clear about its power over me.

She grabbed my right hand and pushed it toward her thighs with some urgency.

"Get in there!" she said. "Get some fingers in my pussy and feel how fucking wet it is."

I reached under her panties and fit one, then two, then three fingers inside her, surrounded by wetness. "Damn!" she said. She had to lean one arm against the massage bed to keep her balance while I worked my fingers in and out.

"See how wet I get?" she said?

"Yes …"

"Jerks who hit on me at bars can never make me wet like this, but a guy like you, who lets me put him in his place … hot damn!"

I felt a flush of embarrassment but also realized my cock twitching to life again.

"Of course, that's nothing compared to how wet I get when"—she was speaking in fragments, as if in a dream—"take me over. Rip the orgasms right out of me!" she commanded, eyes closed, tits swaying. I could almost imagine her riding her lover in ecstasy, tits swaying happily over that lucky man's face—his to touch anytime he wanted.

But not for me. The pain was perfect in its truth.

As if reading my mind, Kristen took my fingers out of her pussy and started putting her pants back on.

"Dammit, I'm gonna be horny the rest of the day," she said, "but it will be worth it." She smiled.

I started to clean up as well. Suddenly I wanted to leave.

I got down from the table, putting my pants on quickly, not caring if I missed a belt loop.

"Jason …" she started.

"Yeah …"

"You're going to experience a lot of emotions after this session. You might even get angry with me. From here on out, the rules change. You make all the appointments, not me. And only when you're ready." She smiled as she put her tank top back on, with a kindness that shocked me given how brutally honest she had been.

"Think of this as my gift to you and the other women in your life."

That line repeated in my head after I left, but the confusion only increased. *A gift for the other women in my life?* I had never felt more insecure about myself, never more inadequate. And I had to pay her for the privilege. *How was this helping me?*

Chapter 10

IT WAS EASY TO hate Kristen a little bit, and so I did. I found myself whaling on the punching bag at the gym. I was so fucking pissed at her—hell, at all the women who had rejected me for reasons fair or unfair. I had been nothing but nice, decent, funny, attentive, *everything women claimed they fucking wanted*!

I swore I would never call her. I felt even more certain of that vow a few days later after a couple more sessions on the punching bag. Who needed to live in a world of addiction and fetish? There had to be another way forward.

A week went by. The horny memories faded; I hit the gym hard. Then, on Thursday morning before work, I saw a girl in the gym I hadn't seen before. I've never been that attracted to "exercise mat" gym girls, but she was not that kind. She looked to be in her mid-twenties and had a black tattoo of a dragon snaking down her right arm. Her hair was short white blonde; the muscles in her arms and back rippled under her skin when she moved. She was half girl, half jungle cat, and she never went near the aerobics room. Yeah, I liked her.

When she went over to the free weights and put twenty-five pounds on each side I kept an eye on her. She pumped out two reps no problem; then she started to slow. I watched her struggling with the last few repetitions, so I ran over, Mr. Helpful.

"Need a spot?" Without waiting for an answer, I put my hands under the bar in case she needed it, but she didn't. She extended her arms fully and racked the bar on her own. When she sat up and toweled her face, she smiled briefly. I was riveted. Later I made a point of walking over to her at the water cooler.

"My name is Jason," I said with my hand extended.

"Hi Jason, I'm Lorrie."

She extended her hand and smiled again, but in a decisive way that made it clear she didn't suffer any fools. I asked about her workout routine, how long she'd been coming to the gym.

She interrupted me mid-sentence. "You know, Jason, I don't do small talk. Let's be clear … I'm not interested, okay?"

I clammed up. She smiled kindly and said, "I'll see you again, I'm sure," before walking away.

Never had I been shut down that efficiently. I felt my cheeks get hot and looked around the gym—casually, as if to survey the equipment, but also to see if anyone had seen me get slammed. Fortunately, it didn't look like anyone had.

The next day, I actually changed my routine in the hopes of not seeing her. Unfortunately she was there. This time she was being spotted by this muscular brown-skinned guy. His arms were pretty big, big enough to make me wonder if he was taking questionable supplements. I knew how hard it was to get to that point.

I was hoping-hoping-HOPING they were just workout partners, but then I saw her bend down and peck him on the lips before grabbing her bag and heading to the locker room. He was shorter than her, so Lorrie had to lean into him. Her mystery man stuck around and lifted some more weights after she was gone, an impressive bench press of three forty-five pound plates on each side—far more reps than I could do. I couldn't help but scan his crotch, wondering what he was giving her. I was relieved to see nothing out of the ordinary. It made me hopeful; maybe if I could bulk up and get in fantastic shape, she would find me as sexy as this guy.

I moved on with my workout. Later, walking through the locker room, I ran into him again changing clothes. He was naked except for some kind of jock strap. Who wears jock straps when they work out? As he was peeling the strap off, a big soft cock flopped out. I didn't want him to get the wrong idea, so I walked into the next section of lockers. *He looked bigger soft than I was hard. Ugh.* The clock on the wall caught my eye. I was about thirty minutes off on schedule. My damn watch must have stopped again. I would need to take a shower here.

I stashed my stuff and walked to the shower. It was just me in the shower and one other older guy with his back to me. I dreaded the group showers here, but there was no time to go home. I soaped up quickly and rinsed, quickly moving to the shampoo and studying the cracks in the brick wall, trying hard not to look at the skinny old dude behind me or think about Lorrie's boyfriend. I hoped like hell that he wouldn't walk in while I was still showering.

Luck wasn't with me.

"Holy shit that's a big dick!" It was the older guy behind me. I knew he wasn't talking to me.

"You like it?" I took a quick glance to my right to see Lorrie's boyfriend entering the showers and hanging his towel up. His dick seemed even a little bigger, maybe enjoying the attention.

I looked away quickly, surprised this guy was so willing to talk to another man about his cock.

"How big does it get?" the older guy asked.

"It's been measured at ten inches," Lorrie's boyfriend said proudly.

I snuck another quick glance at him. I didn't see ten inches but I did see something huge jutting off his body, poking this way and that as he turned the shower on.

"I'd invite you to touch it, but I don't think that's allowed here," Lorrie's boyfriend said.

I thought I heard the older man moan. Oh boy did I want the hell out of here! But I'd have to walk past both of them to do it, and I'd hung my towel on the other side of them to avoid getting it wet. Doh!

I stared hard as ever at the crack that ran between the brown bricks above the shower head.

"I'll bet you've fucked a lot of girls with that big thing," the older guy said.

Lorrie's boyfriend laughed. "I get plenty," he said. "A couple of guys too."

I heard more panting from the older guy's direction. I was afraid to look at him.

"Once I fucked a guy's girlfriend right in front of him, and then I fucked him!" Lorrie's boyfriend said.

I heard some weird slapping noise behind me so I took a quick glance over my left shoulder and saw that the older guy was spanking his own not-small cock.

"Jeezus!" the old guy said. A quick glance to the right, and a view of Lorrie's boyfriend soaping up his nearly-erect cock— by far the biggest I have seen before or since. Most of the cocks I have been impressed are firmly in the "big" category, but this one was enormous.

I was out of there. I walked past them in a hurry clutching my towel, laughter chasing me from behind. It wasn't till I wrapped the towel around me that I realized I was completely erect, which may have been the source of their laughter as they saw me getting the hell out of there but unable to deny … well, I don't know.

I went home with a lot on my mind. Here I was killing myself to work out, trying to become the kind of hot guy girls wanted. But I couldn't seem to get the attention of the girls I was drawn to. Meantime a guy with a big swinging dick seemed to have no problem getting the sex he needed. My rebellion against Kristen suddenly felt like hot air. What other options did I have?

For the first time all week, I thought about her. About how she seemed to have an appreciation for me, *and yes— compassion*. And I thought about how she teased me. And how much I liked it. Checkmate.

"I knew you'd call," she said, happy and cocky in that way I loved and hated.

"Can I … make another appointment?"

"Sure," she said, "I'd love that."

The next afternoon, I was over at her place.

Kristen opened the door dressed in an outfit that was an obvious attempt to torture me—cut-off jeans with a bandana for a belt, sweatshirt with the zipper mostly up and the sleeves cut off. The way her breasts seemed to move inside, I wasn't sure if she had anything on underneath.

She asked me to get ready on the table, no towel. "Lie on your back," she called out. I knew the routine.

As usual I tried like hell to stay calm after I undressed, but it was not to be. Just thinking about the swinging breasts under her sweatshirt was too much.

I had to let it go. She knocked, came in, and immediately started laughing.

"Oh! You're already hard. You must really be looking forward to this appointment." She gave me a stern smile.

"Yeah," I had to admit.

She started with a conventional massage, kneading her way up my legs. As she approached my upper thighs, my cock twitched and hardened further.

She reached for me. "I can never get over how much smaller this dick is than the ones I usually touch. It feels so different in my hand." Her smile was teasing.

"Oh," I said helplessly, moaning with the pleasure. I knew

I wouldn't be able to hold out long, even with this casually stroking.

"So … we're going to have some fun today," Kristen said. "But it's not going to be an easy session for you. The next stages in your education are going to be difficult, I have to warn you now." She spoke forcefully, stroking me more firmly.

With those sensations running through my cock, I was hardly going to leave. I couldn't imagine why the session would be so bad. After all, I was going to cum and come hard.

"I want to start by asking you why, after our last appointment, you made this one."

I almost made up some story about how I missed her, but I knew I had to tell her the truth. So I told her about the gym and the hot tattooed blond girl, how she shut me down so completely. And how she showed up the next day with a stud.

"And how did that make you feel?" she asked, continuing to stroke me.

"Small," I said.

"What else?" Kristen asked.

I hesitated. "Inadequate."

"Good. You're being brutally honest with yourself right now. This is really going to help us. What else?"

I thought for a minute.

"Desperate."

"Yeah, she said," stroking me casually. "That's a good word for it."

"Does it bother you that he probably hit on her like you did, or even if he did, that she probably gave in?"

"Yeah."

"You realize she probably hit on him, right? Either because she saw his big dick, heard about it, or because there was just, you know, something about him?"

"Yeah."

"You saw how confident he was, right?"

"Yeah."

"Girls can't resist that. We say we hate cocky guys, but what we hate is false bravado"

"But some guys, there's a … vibe. When you can sense he can back it up—*that* kind of guy—he makes us sooo wet. The first time I had that experience was right after high school," she continued, always stroking, as if her touching me sexually was completely natural. "I was playing hard to get with my boyfriend. I had dated him three months and only let him finger me. Then one night we went to a college party and I fucked a frat boy that same night. It was incredible. I couldn't help myself. Something about him, the way he moved, the way he looked at me. Like he knew he could make my pussy cum because he had made a lot of other pussies cum. All he gave me was a chance to be his slut for one night … and I took it. I got my brains fucked out by his big cock."

Her smile was dreamy now, nostalgic. "He was so much bigger than my boyfriend," she went on. "My boyfriend was sweet and considerate, but tentative. This guy … he just *ravaged* my pussy, completely owned it. Took it over!"

I didn't want to cum yet, but I couldn't help myself, thinking about a guy who could get Kristen on her back that fast, spreading her legs wantonly, cheating without much, if any, regret. I started cumming all over my belly.

"Ha!" Kristen said. "Tiny dicks come so quickly!"

I felt shame when she said that, but the orgasm felt so good it was more than worth it.

"We're going to have to keep working on that," Kristen said, reaching for a towel.

"What?" I asked.

"Your staying power," she said. "Or what you can do when you cum fast."

I was red-faced, but could offer no argument. Clearly it was a lesson I hadn't learned yet.

She used a towel to remove all traces of cum.

"We're not done yet, so I want you cleaned up for the next part," she said.

Not done yet? What else?

After she dried me off, she looked at my cock as if inspecting it.

"It's really fucking tiny when it's small, huh? We need to get it hard again somehow."

Somehow, as it turned out, involved her slowly unzipping and removing her sweatshirt—yes, there was a bra after all—and then her cutoffs. Her black lace bra and panties were all that that was left, and she was quite a sight. She sat down on the table with her back to me.

"Unsnap my bra," she commanded. I struggled with the zipper, causing her to giggle. But then it came off. When she turned around, I could see her breasts hanging confidently in front of her. I was torn between wanting to fuck her brains out and fearing she was way too much woman for me.

I got the sense she was looking at my face the whole time, gauging my reaction.

"What do you think?" she asked, standing before me for inspection like a goddess consulting her slave.

"Oh my god," I said helplessly. "You're so beautiful."

She kneeled toward me, thigh muscles rippling, aware of the power of her hips.

"Put your fingers in my pussy. Feel how wet I am."

I dutifully stuck in two fingers. They went right into her moistness. She was sopping wet.

"You know why I'm so wet?" she asked.

"Because you put me in my place?"

"Exactly! But I have bigger plans for you." With that, she took a look at my dick. It was rock hard solid again, as if it had never cum in the first place.

She hopped off the mat, walked over to a small table in the corner and opened the drawer. She peered over her shoulder, checking to see if I was staring at her ass, which I was. I thought

I saw a flash of anger, but then she smiled, walked back to the table holding something.

It turned out to be a condom.

"I got a package of small condoms today, for little guys," she said.

I felt a rush of heat suffuse my face.

"Usually I buy large condoms, and the checkout girls seem jealous or at least interested in my purchase. This time I got a different look."

She smiled at me, slowly rolling the condom onto my erect cock.

"But it was worth it, because this is the next phase in your education, and I couldn't risk a condom falling off your little cock when you're in my pussy," she said wickedly.

I found myself twitching in her hands, loving her touch. *In my pussy?* Hadn't she told me before I would never, ever fuck her?

"So are you ready to fuck me?" she asked.

"Yes!" I said without any hesitation.

"You really want inside this pussy, don't you?"

"Oh god, yes!"

"Well, I haven't had a dick that small inside my pussy for a very long time, and back then I was practically a virgin," she teased. "So if you want to get inside this pussy, you're going to have to beg me for it."

With that, she got on the table and straddled me, rubbing my cock to remind me who was in charge. Then she slid the condom onto my cock.

"A nice, 'snug' fit—just like it says on the box!" she said, laughing.

I was crazy hard, but she wouldn't put me inside her. Instead she stroked me in front of her pussy, sometimes rubbing me against her lips.

"Please ... please let me fuck you!" I hated how desperate

that sounded, but I wanted it so bad. I didn't want to cum first and ruin this chance.

Without missing a beat, she raised her pussy up above my cock, teasing it a bit, brushing past the opening and raising up again.

"You really want to fuck me?"

"God, yes!"

"Then beg me to put that tiny dick inside me, since my pussy is used to so much more."

"Oh, please!" I said.

She smiled and rubbed up against me, pressing my cock against her belly.

"Only if you beg me," she said.

"God I'll do anything!" I said, thrusting up toward her, but she had my cock pressed down against my belly. I wasn't getting in without her approval.

"Jason, you have to really beg me to put this substandard cock inside my beautiful pussy!"

"Oh, please, put my little dick inside you!"

"Getting closer." Suddenly I knew what I had to say. And that I had to say it loud.

"Please put my tiny dick inside you!" I practically yelled. A smug look of approval from Kristen.

"Okay, but be careful what you wish for."

With that, she put my dick inside her and slid all the way down on it in one motion.

She moved up and down to get the feel of it before removing her left hand from the base of my cock.

"See how easily this fits inside me?" she asked.

"Yeah …" I said.

"This is a problem for girls. We want friction. What I feel with you inside me is … pleasant, but it's subtle, more like a concentration exercise than a mind-blowing experience."

As she said it, she started to ride up and down. "Let's see if I can feel you any better if we move faster." She was quiet as she closed her eyes in concentration. "With a big dick inside me, at this point, I'm still struggling to get it in, to adjust to its thickness."

She started bouncing up and down more vigorously. I reached up and grabbed her tits, trying to caress them like she had taught me. But she pushed my hands away, as if distracted.

Then she started slamming into me hard … but my cock slipped out. She guided it back in and got back into thrusting, but I slipped out again.

"This is the other problem," she said. "Not only am I having trouble getting friction, but I can't keep the motion going. With a nice big cock, I can ride up and down and still have a lot of cock to spare for long thrusts. That means I'm constantly getting massaged way up inside me, no matter where he is in the thrusting motion—no breaks, no slips, just pure fucking rhythm!" She licked her lips. "And that's what makes a pussy cum. With a little dick like yours, it's better just to grind, not to bounce. I'll show you what I mean."

She took me all the way inside her and ground into me strongly, pubic bone on bone.

"Ohh …" I said.

"Does that feel good?" she asked.

"Oh yeah!" I said.

"See, that's the problem," she said, leaning over me, letting her hair cover my face and her breasts rest on my chest.

"Problem?" I said. It felt incredible.

"It feels amazing to you, but to me, well, I really don't feel anything much. We could do this for an hour, and it would never make me cum," she said. "Well, maybe not for an hour," she said and laughed. "You'd cum way before then."

"But what if I worked your clit while we were fucking?" I asked hopefully.

"Well, that might work, but that's a different kind of cum," She explained. "It's a clit orgasm, not a deep vaginal body cum.

Let's see if your little dick can last five minutes inside my hot pussy."

She sat back upright, grinding on me in a circular motion, really letting her hips move around the base of my cock. So much so that I almost fell out again, but she pulled me right back inside her and kept moving.

I couldn't help myself. In just a couple minutes I was cumming, spurting up into the condom. She was totally in control. She started to laugh.

As soon as I came, I felt this wave of despair and nausea sweep through me. Why was I subjecting myself to this? I felt like a virgin who had failed to please a princess and was now condemned to be locked in the stocks.

A couple of tears welled up. Her face instantly softened …

"Oh honey, that's okay, that's okay, let it out." She kissed me on the lips and cheek, still holding my cock inside her. She had compassion for me, but she was not sorry. She was the furthest thing from sorry.

"You're a great man, a brave man. You just … have some sexual learning to do. I'm not just going to break you down, you'll see."

I hate to write it, but I cried some more.

"You do like fucking me, don't you?"

"Yes," I said.

"That's good," she said. "You'll look back on this night, and you'll remember how hot it was, not how sad.

"Mmmm," she added. "I haven't had this much fun with a man in a long time."

"Fun?" I repeated.

"Yeah … Usually guys are way too tied to their egos to let themselves go like you have. I love it!"

With that, she stepped off the massage table. I assumed it was over, that she would be reaching for her clothes. But she didn't.

"How's that little dick of yours doing?" she asked me

playfully, teasing me with her right hand. I was rock hard again ... already. Just talking about my predicament had brought my dick around again.

"Okay, so I have to tell you, this next part isn't going to be easy for you either, but it's really important," she said as she stroked. "If you go along with this, it will help you, and then I promise you a fantastic orgasm. Fair enough?"

"Okay," I said, unsure. But there was no looking back.

"Now, for the next few minutes, I'm going to act a little different, like a girl who is desperate to be fucked ... okay?"

"Okay," I said again, wondering where this was headed.

"Stand up now," she said in that commanding voice that always put me in motion. I stood.

With that, she leaned against the door and stuck her ass out at me, moving her fingers up and down her pussy lips.

"Oh, god, I need a good fucking," she said, moving fingers in and out while rotating her ass. I had never seen anything as hot as her gorgeous tan ass from behind. Or as demanding.

"Get over here and fuck me!" she said, looking back at me almost angrily.

I did as I was told, standing behind her, trying to work my cock in. But she was standing at a tough angle, and truth be told, she was taller than me. I moved the tip of my cock against her pussy lips, but her ass was moving, and I couldn't get it in.

"C'mon, fuck me!" she said, her voice loud and insistent.

I tried again to get my cock up in her, but with her ass moving around, even though I was rock hard, she was just out of reach. I was starting to get embarrassed.

"Dammit! Your cock is too small to fuck me like that. I really need it, too... Let's try something else."

This time she leaned over the edge of the massage table, sticking her ass up in the air for me.

"Fuck it! Pleeeasssse." She looked back at me, in heat but angry.

I got behind her. From this angle I was able to kind of get

my cock head in after a few false starts and more sighs of impatience from her.

Not wanting to risk falling out, I pushed myself up into her until I was at the base.

"That's it. Put it in deeper, give me more …"

I knew I was in all the way, so I tried to ignore that and concentrate on the effortless sway of her body. I started pounding her.

"Yes," she said, "give it to me harder!"

Gaining confidence, I grabbed her waist and started pounding her as hard as I could. I was really in a rhythm and could hear her moaning loader as the base of my dick slapped against her ass. I was really doing it!

But then she started pushing her ass out at me harder and moving it around a bit, trying to get in deeper. Even concentrating on my strokes, I slipped out. I reached down and got it back in and started pounding again, but she was really getting into the motion and I quickly fell out.

"Put it back in there!" she said insistently. I tried, but I was starting to get nervous and I couldn't find her entrance easily with her ass moving in the air. I tried, and failed. Tried and failed.

Sighing again, she reached back and guided it in herself. I started pounding again, but again when she bucked her hips against me, I fell out.

"Damnit!" she said. "It's no use."

She rolled over again, rubbing her pussy. "And I needed to get fucked so bad."

"I can do it to you on here!" I said, climbing on the bed. She pushed me off.

"I don't think you understand," she said. "I needed to get fucked, really taken, taken by force from behind. But your tiny dick kept falling out."

"I know I can fuck you from the top position," I said insistently.

"Okay," she said with a bit of resignation.

I got on top of her, amazed at the view from above, the sweat rolling off her breasts and face.

I put myself inside her and started pushing.

"Yeah," I said, unable to help myself.

"Does that feel good?" she said, almost glaring up at me.

"Yeah!" I said, stroking inside her amazing pussy, not believing my good fortune.

"Because I can't really feel much," she said. "Oh well, I'm glad you feel something."

I started pounding her harder, but she reached up and grabbed my waist and slowed me down again.

"Don't bother," Kristen said. "It's not going to make me cum, and that wasn't really the point of this anyhow."

"So what was the point?"

"I'll show you next week," Kristen said, unceremoniously taking my dick out of her. All of a sudden, she was uninterested in me and my orgasm.

"Go ahead and get dressed, and I'll see you next week. I'm going to take a shower," she added matter-of-factly. Then she turned toward me. "I want to remember exactly what we did today, how it made me feel, how it made you feel." She wrapped her body in a towel and walked out. I could hear her shower sputter up in the distance.

After she left the massage room, I stood there alone, my cock rock hard, my balls aching. I put my erection back in my jeans, feeling mad at her and also humiliated. I honestly wasn't sure I would call her again. In that moment, I thought, *Probably never*.

Chapter 11

I DID CALL KRISTEN again. Eventually.

Truth is I struggled with this, asked myself if it was self-destructive, asked myself if it was a hopeless addiction fed by the most confused parts of myself. To this day I can't tell you with any certainty it wasn't one of those things, all those things. What I will say in my defense is that I continued to try to find something better. I had started to fundamentally question whether Kristen had my best interests at heart. She had promised to break me down and she was well on the way. But to what end?

So I tried. I asked out a few girls I kind of liked. I had to force the issue a bit, as I didn't have a huge crush on these women. Years ago, my grandfather of all people had advised me that sometimes you "fall in like" with someone first, and then you fall in love. That love was more about being there, companionship, and the other feelings that grow over time. "Quit looking for Mrs. Perfect while other guys go marry Mrs. Good Enough," was how he unromantically put it.

In my mid-twenties now, I was starting to see his point. More women that I had some kind of interest in were either engaged or married. For the first time I could see how you pay a price for waiting for the perfect situation. Although I wasn't really waiting for perfect. I just wanted someone who could reach inside my heart and shake me. Maybe that *was* a search for perfection. Kristen had no problem doing that to me. But with her I faced a different challenge—mutuality of feeling. She loved me but I LOVED her. That discrepancy was brutal.

So after that last meeting, I tried to date. Tried. But my heart wasn't in it. I found myself staring across a dinner table listening to an attractive woman talk about her career plans— law versus business, corporate law versus advertising if you really want to know—and I just couldn't see myself in her life. Each woman was nice in her own way but none of them grabbed me by the jugular.

I suppose on some level I had outgrown *nice*. I had come to crave truth. Nice felt phony and truth was a relief. Truth I could work with. Speaking of which, while Marilyn (our career planner) was talking, I found myself looking forward to being back in bed alone, where my thoughts often turned to … Kristen.

A full month had gone by since our last "incident", which is how I had taken to referring to these encounters. The flat-out truth is that I was worried to let too much time pass, to let whatever strange opportunity I had with her pass me by. I called her, left a voicemail. "I want to continue." I liked that — cryptic and mysterious.

I didn't hear back for two days. Three. I was starting to wonder if that particular train had left. But on the third day, she called.

"Can you meet me at Regina's gym, ten p.m. tonight?"

The time was odd. So was the place. Regina was a friend of hers who had a small gym she used for her clients who were rehabilitating from workplace injuries. I guess they had some kind of "client swap" thing going with the massage work.

Of course I said yes.

Regina's gym was in the basement of a small shopping complex. It was a dark, private location with no windows. In fact, about three months after this particular story, she ended up moving it to a storefront with way more light. But the privacy was what Kristen was looking for, I guess.

When I arrived, I had to knock a few times to be heard from the back entrance. Kristen came out, wearing a tight-fitting spandex outfit and leotard. She looked as hot as you would expect, though to be honest it was the dresses that really knocked me out. But anytime someone is completely at ease in their own physicality, you have to take notice.

Walking into the door of the gym, a big surprise awaited me. We were not alone.

"This is Jim," Kristen said. I gave Jim a once-over. He was a big strapping guy, but kind of a lunk, a cross between Mr. Big on *Sex and the City* with George Costanza on *Seinfeld*. He was taller than me but kind of awkward, and certainly out of place in a gym. Jim was not in particularly good shape. If anything he had a pot belly and the physical look of a guy who would rather suck down a six pack with his pals than get up the next morning and jog with co-workers. Jim seemed like a bit of a creep, and he gave me a funny look.

What was I supposed to do, shake his hand? It looked like Jim was about to extend his hand to break the awkwardness.

"Jim's going to be fucking me today," Kristen said. "And you're going to be watching … well, mostly watching." They both snickered at this inside joke and looked over at me, standing awkwardly, unsure of what to do.

"We picked this gym because no one is here at this time of night and, well, I'm going to be making a lot of noise," Kristen said, smiling knowingly at Jim. They both laughed and looked at me.

"Oh and yes, this is very much part of your instruction," she added. My cheeks flamed.

And with that, she kneeled submissively before him

and started massaging and rubbing a growing bulge in his sweatpants.

"Wait till you see this," she said, looking at me.

She struggled to get out whatever was underneath. Then she pulled out this long, thick rope of a cock, which hung down obscenely. To this day, I have never seen a bigger soft cock. It was maybe seven inches, thick and arrogant. And uncut. Kristen sighed audibly when she saw it, and she had seen it plenty of times before.

When I first saw Jim's penis, I imagined it must be a foot long erect. With Kristen kneeling in front of him stroking it, I was about to find out. What surprised me was how she behaved with him. She was actually whacking her face with his soft cock, playing with it carelessly as she looked up at him admiringly.

Little by little, that soft cock got hard in her hands. To my surprise, it didn't get much longer, but it sure as heck got harder. And thick. Kristen was spitting on it, rubbing it quickly. To be honest I was surprised Jim didn't cum. I thought I saw him moan in pre-orgasm a couple of times, but he steadied himself on a Nautilus handle and she kept on working his dick, his ill-fitting white t-shirt still in place, his sweatpants around his legs.

I had not seen an uncircumcised dick before. Kristen seemed to love messing with the head of it and working it back and forth.

It had been a long time since I'd had the chance to watch a girl have sex in front of me. I was feeling a little weak in the knees at the prospect. I sat down on a bench near the bench press.

I was chagrined, hoping that he would have trouble getting as hard as me, but no: his cock was not only hard, but it even pointed upward a bit, despite the weight. It looked pretty goddamn intimidating. Maybe to her, too?

"Jim, I need to get fucked," Kristen said. I don't think I've ever seen a girl strip so fast. Kristen slipped out of her leotard in one quick movement and pulled her tights off so aggressively I thought they might rip.

Jim kicked off his shoes and shrugged out of his shirt as well. It was weird to watch his transformation from big awkward oaf to "man in charge." His cock jutted outward with authority— way more Mr. Big than George Costanza now.

"Come here," Jim called out to her, and she approached, obediently, putting his arms around her waist. "You're not ready for this big cock yet," he said to her in his gravelly voice.

"Oh yes I am. I want it!" said Kristen.

"We have to get you wetter first," he said. With that, he started working a couple of his fingers inside her pussy. The look on her face was a jolt, like a light socket being switched on.

"Oh god," Kristen said. "Oh god."

It seemed like she had even forgotten I was here, rubbing my cock through my pants. No one cared what I did, at least for now.

Kristen had grabbed Jim's cock in her left hand and was stroking it, or attempting to, while she alternately thrust into and away from his hands, as if the pleasure was too intense.

"God you know how to work me," she cooed. Then she surprised me by quickly pulling him to her and kissing him hard.

It was tough to watch that kiss. It wasn't the rough quickie I was hoping for, but a real soulful kiss that made me feel more like I was watching a couple on their wedding night.

God I wanted that kiss to end.

After what seemed like a damned eternity, he finally pulled his mouth away from hers. But they stayed in a close embrace.

"Oh god, I can feel your huge cock all up against my belly!" Kristen said, pulling him even closer with her strong arms around his back.

"Yeah, that feels good to me too, Kristen," Jim said seductively. "Just think how good it's going to feel all up inside you."

"Oh god!" Kristen said. It seemed like she was thrusting up into him. No way could she take his cock from that angle, but she was clearly pushing her pussy right up onto it.

"Oh yeah, you're wet enough now," Jim said. "Look!"

And with that he stepped back. Even from ten feet away I could see the pussy juice running down her legs. His cock was also glistening, maybe not any longer but as hard as I had ever seen a cock. Damn that dick was thick. I couldn't imagine a girl taking it without serious pain.

But Kristen didn't seem to care. She went over and leaned against a Nautilus shoulder press bench, bracing herself against the cushion. With the other hand, she opened up her pussy and leaned back, humping her ass in the air. Then something unexpected happened. She actually remembered I was there.

"Come closer!" she ordered. I sat down on a weight bench about eight feet away, but with a better side angle, where I would really be able to see them.

"No, Jason, pull the bench closer!" Kristen said. It was intense to hear her say my name in the middle of this. In a really bizarre way, I felt like I mattered to her. That I was being included. That I was lucky she was sharing this with me. From the first time I had seen her bedroom, I'd had horribly wicked dreams about what she got up to in there. I was about to find out.

"Now, Jim!" She glared at him. He knew exactly what to do, moving in on her quickly.

"Watch closely, Jason!" she told me.

I suddenly realized the significance of this scene. She was setting herself up to get fucked *in the exact same position* that we had tried and failed at a month before. Jim leaned over her and she moved her hips wantonly. I heard a loud "plop" as his uncut mushroom head popped into her. I suddenly realized she had not made him wear a condom. If I was her boyfriend, I would have protested. But I was not. Not even close.

"Wow!" she said. She tried to pull back instinctively, but

before she could, he inserted another couple inches of cock inside her, keeping her impaled as he pulled her ass back toward him.

"Wow!" she said.

Slowly but surely, careful not to thrust too hard and give her too much length, he started moving a few inches in and out of her.

"Damnnnnnn," she said.

"You're really tight tonight, baby," he said in her ear. She smiled and looked back at him.

"It's because I haven't had your big dick inside me for three days," she said, with a petulant look on her face.

"I'll make it up to you tonight, okay, sweetie?" he said softly, giving her a brief kiss.

"Yeahhhh," she said.

Jim increased the pace of his thrusts, still just a few inches in and out, in and out. I found myself amazed she could take even that much, but then I remembered how wet she was.

"Ohhhhh," Kristen said, and I could see her pussy lips clinging to his cock outside her body on each thrust. I realized what Jim's physical advantage was. In this position, he could work a few inches inside her, getting her warmed up, with almost no risk of falling out or interrupting the rhythm. What would that do to her?

"You're such a slut," he teased.

"No I'm not!" she objected. "I'm just a girl who gets what she wants."

"No, you're a slut for my cock, and I'll prove it to you."

With that, he rammed himself almost all the way inside her and grabbed her shoulders.

"I'm fucking you now …" he said, and he meant it.

He started moving in and out with determination, not slamming her, but leaving about an inch outside on each thrust.

As I rubbed myself—now totally hard under my own pants—I could see Jim was at no risk of falling out even as

Kristen moved her ass around. The best part, for her anyway, was that at least a few inches of his dick were in her pussy at all times, even as he pulled out. That must feel amazing to her, I thought.

As if reading my mind, she said, "Oh baby, that feels so amazing."

It was awesome to watch her push that muscular back in the air and know she was getting exactly what she craved, *even if it wasn't from me.*

As for Jim, he appeared to be in no rush, just moving in and out of her strongly, but with no real urgency.

"Oh Jim, if you keep doing that, you're gonna make my pussy cum!" Kristen said.

I looked more closely; I thought I could see the beginnings of a tremble or a ripple in her body as she moved.

It must be incredible, I thought, letting yourself go into an orgasm. If the guy just keeps it up, your pleasure is inevitable.

"Oh, you ain't seen nothing yet," Jim said.

"Ohhhhhhh, she groaned as he thrust a little harder but still in rhythm.

"That's it," Kristen said. "I'm cumming!" And she did. I could see her body shake and tremble as he pulled her ass back into him, keeping his cock buried inside her while her orgasms rippled through. Without even realizing it, I had pulled my own hard cock out of my zipper, stroking openly. Neither one of them had even noticed.

"Oh baby, that was so good," Kristen said, reaching back to brush his face and hair sweetly.

They were still fucking, but very slowly, tenderly even. As Kristen caught her breath, she looked over at me.

"Did you see that?" she said. I nodded.

"I see you liked it," she said. I stopped suddenly, ashamed, perhaps flashing back to the time I'd peeped on Beth.

"No, don't stop, Jason," Kristen said. "I want you to stroke your little dick while you watch me fuck." I thought I heard Jim laugh quietly.

"You know why I wanted you to see this," Kristen said.

I nodded.

"So stroke it," she said. "Make it feel good."

Jim pulled his dick out of her, and her pussy exhaled with a loud obscene plop that made them both laugh again. He grabbed her hand and walked her over the side of a leg press. He placed both her hands at the top of the press and stood behind her, adjusting her ass outward. Without waiting for permission, he started easing his cock back inside her. I was amazed at how easy it was for him to insert his cock in this "standing up" position. When Kristen and I had tried that position, it had been a physical impossibility. I felt a surge of inadequacy and excitement, watching him bend her head down as she willingly complied.

"Hey, Jason ..." It was the first time Jim had spoken to me directly. "Do you want to see Kristen act like a total slut?"

"Hey!" Kristen said, looking back at him, faux-angry.

"You want to see what a dirty fucking whore she really is?"

"Jim!" Kristen said, trying to pull away from him, but he was holding his cock inside her and her smaller body was pressed up against him. She had nowhere to go ... not that she really wanted to.

"Yeah," I said without further hesitation.

"Jason!" Kristen said to me in that mock angry tone that you didn't want to hear from her, in case real anger was around the corner.

"Okay, you asked for it," Jim said. With that, he slammed his cock inside her.

The next ten minutes are difficult to describe. It all happened so fast, with such mesmerizing intensity. What I can tell you is that I've never seen anyone get fucked so hard.

Turns out the first standing position was more like foreplay. This was the real thing. Jim was slamming his cock inside her continuously. Her pussy was making crazy slushing sounds as her ass slapped up against his cock. He had her mostly by the shoulders, pulling her into him. It looked to me like she was coming continuously, bucking her ass all over the place. I envied his big cock. With my small one, there was no hope I could have kept it inside her while she was wildly bucking around like that. I don't think the air was on in the gym after hours. Her hair was caked to her face and her back was glistening with sweat.

Yeah, she looked pretty much like a slut. Of course for me that meant she looked beautiful, perfect. It was like they were born to please each other.

Then a surprise: Jim took his cock out of her and slapped it a few times on her ass. It was amazing to see how much noise his big cock could make, all red and shiny and slick with her cum. It sounded like he was whopping her back with a paddle.

"Oh, why'd you take it out?" she whined, bucking her ass in an effort to find his cock. "I was just about to cum …"

Had she really said '*just* about to cum'? Then what was the body shaking she had been doing for the last few minutes?

"Because if you want this, you have to beg for it."

"Oh pleeeeeease …" Kristen said, pushing her ass back up at him, "Please put it back inside me."

"Are you my slut?" he demanded.

"Oh god, yes!" she said.

"Tell Jason you're my slut. Tell him you're a slut for my big dick!"

"Jason, yes," she said, "sorry, but I just can't help it. I'm such a fucking slut for his big cock!"

That seemed to satisfy Jim. As he inserted his cock back inside her, she made happy moaning sounds. Her breasts swayed underneath her. As much as I wanted her to myself and felt the surge of jealousy to prove it, there was no denying that *I loved watching her being conquered like this, all her brashness reduced to submission.*

Jim grabbed her hair roughly and just started pounding her. "Fuck me back!" he commanded.

And she did, pushing her ass back on him whenever he pulled too far away. She quickly pulled a bench over to brace her legs up so she could steady herself, bending her knees as needed.

"Oh fuck me!" she yelled. "Just fuck me!!!"

Jim was working it. I couldn't believe he was able to fuck so long without coming.

"Cum for me," Jim said. "Get what you need!"

He slowed his thrusts but they didn't miss a beat. She was pushing back at him so hard and screaming and yelling and I could see her body shaking from her ass up to her head.

"Oh god, yeah, I'm gonna FUCKING CUM SO FUCKING HARD!! GOD, YOUR COCK IS SO FUCKING BIG!! OH MY GOOOOODDD!!!

I could understand now why she wanted a private space. It sounded like she was screaming for her life. But as I can attest, it was not agony but its flip side, rapture.

At just the right time, Jim reached down to Kristen's legs and pulled her to him. Her whole body trembled and shook for what seemed like a minute. Spit even fell from her chin as she gasped for breath.

"Oh yeah, baby, your pussy's gonna squirt!"

"Oh fuck, IT IS!!" she screamed.

With a loud squish, Jim's cock was out of Kristen's pussy as if she'd expelled it. Expertly, Jim reached between Kristen's legs and worked her pussy lips, as if to empty them, and while Kristen held her hips up, I could see spurts of her fluid surging out of her pussy onto Jim's hand, onto the ground, everywhere.

"We got a squirter!!" Jim called over to me triumphantly, claiming it like he would a trophy. Clearly he had seen this kind of thing before. I had never seen a pussy squirt at all, much less jets of fluid the way a cock did.

"Now we're gonna fuck!" Jim said, moving Kristen gently

off him and lying down on the bench. She straddled him and lowered himself down, inch by inch, totally focused on her primal urge. I was fascinated by how her pussy lips extended and gripped his thick cock, struggling to accommodate him before finally working most of it in. Her happy sighs told me all I needed to know about how that kind of fullness must have felt. They fucked for a few minutes that way before Jim sat up and, without pulling his cock out, stood and started bouncing her around on him.

"Let me give you a good view, Jason," Jim said generously, walking a few steps as she held onto his shoulders. When her back was a few feet in front of me, he raised her up and down, and you could see again what an advantage his long dick had. He moved her up and down and never came close to flopping out. From this angle, her weight could slam into him, taking him deeply but not deeper than she could handle. The advantage of his thickness was undeniable as well; you could hear the loud plunging sounds caused by so much deep friction.

It was inevitable she would cum with that kind of fucking, and cum she did, shaking and trembling and sweating while he held her tight, letting her get all the cum out of her body.

It may sound crazy, but I felt a debt of gratitude to him. I was so happy to see her so blissful. You have to understand. I knew her struggles, her hard times growing up, some of her ups and downs in her personal life. She might have been a force in the world but it didn't mean her life had been easy. She needed this. She deserved it. When Jim released her, she stood on wobbly legs, propping herself against him. Kristen looked so relieved and so … fucked out.

But Jim wanted to show me a little more. He seemed to understand why I was here as much as she did. He sat down again on the bench and guided Kristen to sit down on him, facing me. It was stunning to watch the look on her face as she sank down onto his dick. You could see even after all this sex that it still wasn't easy for her to take him in.

Kristen controlled the action this time, riding slowly up and down on his cock, obviously a bit weary from the intense sex she had already received, enjoying a pleasurable but relaxing fuck. I realized she was now paying more attention to me. Smiling in a knowing way, kind of mean, as if I was lucky to be there. Maybe I was. She beckoned me over.

"Come closer," she motioned.

I did.

"Hold me up so I can really fuck him," she demanded, motioning for me to stand behind her. I did as I was told.

"My legs are too weak from fucking," Kristen said. Then she tilted her chin upward and smiled firmly at me. "Help me move up and down on his huge cock so I can cum again."

I had never felt anything quite so humiliating ... or erotic. I braced her with my arms and started moving her up and down. It seemed to help, as she started fucking him faster, leaning a bit on my side but still angled well enough to fuck. I'm not sure I ever felt more certain of my sexual place. It was here. *With her. Helping her cum so damn hard.* Feeling her lean on me while she fucked, trusting me to hold her. It was one of the more intimate things I had ever done with a woman, and certainly the most taboo.

Damn! I kept trying to pull her higher, higher than his dick could reach, but Jim expertly adjusted his thrusts to match. He seemed to be enjoying my efforts. I could see him grin over at me before he went back to thrusting.

Thanks to my arm strength, Kristen was able to use what was left of her shaky leg muscles, rising up and letting her weight fall. Suddenly I felt a slight tremor go through her, then another.

"Did you feel that?" She twisted and looked up at me with urgency.

"Yeah!" I said. It was amazing to feel that vibration, like the first ripples of a massive earthquake.

The earthquake hit. "Oh my god!!" Kristen said, sitting down on him and rocking her way through an orgasm. She held my hands down to prevent me from pulling her up while she shook all over. His dick was still entirely inside her. I was so happy for her, and unbelievably jealous. *And hard as a fucking rock.*

Then something happened that has never happened before or since. I started to squirt. Without any contact from my hand or anyone else's. Just cumming ... onto her back and shoulder and neck. I expected Kristen to freak out but she was too distracted by the remaining burst of her orgasms.

She panted and sighed for a couple of minutes, letting that huge orgasm seep out of her body but never raising herself off his dick. I heard her giggle and motion me around to her left side.

Then she took a good look at me.

"Did your tiny dick squirt all over me?" she asked, giggling.

"Yeah." I could only confess. But I added quickly, "I wasn't even touching it!"

"Wait ... you mean you came on me without even stroking?"

"Yeah."

"Wow. You must really love watching me fuck!"

"Yeah." I was getting better at responding to her promptly. She seemed pleased.

"Grab your shirt and clean me up!" she demanded.

I grabbed the shirt off the Nautilus rack. I'm not sure why I didn't get a towel from the towel bin, but for some reason it seemed right to use my shirt for this. *Like the dirty boy you are,* her voice rang out in my head.

I lovingly cleaned the cum off her back.

Jim had propped himself up on his right elbows, watching us like we were on a late night cable movie you probably shouldn't be watching.

"You really do love watching me fuck and cum, don't you?"

"Yes," I said again.

She made a hum of approval.

"Well, here's another great thing about Jim's big cock. He's not even hard anymore, and he's still up inside me, giving me pleasure." Kristen rotated a bit on his cock.

"See that?" Kristen said.

"Yeah," I said.

"You had trouble staying inside of me even when you were hard, didn't you?"

I nodded.

"You'd have no chance if you were soft, would you?" she pressed.

"No." I admitted.

"But then again, you're not soft now, are you?" she said, smiling up.

It was true. Something about this scene … I couldn't stop looking at her fuck. My dick was ready for more, in record time.

With that, she stepped off Jim's cock and beckoned for him to stand across from me, angling us both toward her.

"Let's see who cums first," Kristen said wickedly. Ugh, I could almost sense the pending humiliation. But I knew she wasn't doing this out of curiosity; *she was doing this for me*. She knew exactly how to get me off. It was one of the things that convinced me I loved her—in that forbidden way cuckolds know so intimately.

Even though I had already cum once, I didn't see myself lasting long in this scenario. And that's exactly what she had in mind. She carefully peeled the condom off Jim's cock and tossed it aside, looking at his big hanging dick in appreciation.

She put a hand on each of our cocks and started working them, sliding up and down.

Just like the time in college with Zach, the difference was striking. Jim's cock was almost bigger than her grip and she had to move her arm up and back to cover the distance.

"I only need a couple fingers for yours," Kristen said, smiling at me.

Ugh. But my cock twitched hard.

"It's amazing," Kristen said, pulling us a bit closer together. "It's almost like you're two different genders. Or," she added, looking up at me cruelly. "You're the boy, and he's … the man," she stroked us harder, "the man who gets to fuck my pussy … anytime he wants." She looked up at him with utter devotion.

"And you, Jason, you only got to fuck my pussy once, and that was to teach you a lesson." She looked up at me sternly, as if scolding me for even attempting to fuck her. That was it for me. I started spurting all over this goddess of a woman who had put me in my place.

"Tiny dicks cum first!" Kristen said, laughing. "Your tiny dick just squirted!" Jim forgot to be polite and started laughing his ass off too. He seemed so proud of his sexual advantage and what it did for him. I knew I was beet red. I wasn't sure if she was going to laugh again. Now she almost looked disgusted.

She immediately turned her attention to Jim's cock, working both hands up and down on it. I started backing away, thinking this was a good time for me to exit. But Kristen had other ideas.

"Oh no you don't, little boy," she said to me. "I want you to see this."

I stood there dutifully as she proceeded to wank him off with both hands, faster and faster.

I thought surely he would cum with that kind of intense rubbing, but no, he held out, moaning, eyes closed, enjoying the sensation. For another five minutes she worked both hands furiously up and down his cock, aggressively trying to make it cum. But it didn't. His cock was dripping pre-cum the whole time, so she would wipe the cum from his mushroom head and lube the rest of his cock with it. Soon he was wet and slick and shiny.

"God it's so hard to make you cum!!" she said, working him faster. "That really turns me on, you know that?" She glanced over at me to compare us. Then she went back to her intense jerking motions.

"Jeezus that's a big fucking cock! So full of cum!!!" Kristen said. "I can't believe how well you fuck!"

Not even Jim was immune to such teasing talk. I thought I could see his dick twitching.

With some authority, Kristen kneeled in front of Jim. She was back in sexual control again, no longer in his thrall. She reached her left hand under his dangling, heavy balls while continuing to stroke his cock with her right hand.

"Oh!" Jim groaned. Kristen seemed to recognize the moment.

"Look at this," Kristen said, nodding me closer. "That's it, baby," she said to Jim. "Show him how a real man cums." That one hurt.

"Oh!!" Jim said.

"That's it," Kristen said. Jim spurted a couple of times.

"Oh!" he said again. And that was it.

I was relieved. He had managed just a few small spurts, even more half-hearted than mine, which at least had landed on Kristen's tits.

As if reading my thoughts, Kristen said to me, "Keep watching."

Her stroking and rubbing was too much for Jim. Suddenly rope after rope of thick cum came spurting out of his cock, each one more vigorous than the last.

I thought Kristen would think it was gross, but it seemed to really turn her on. Jim's ass clenched as he kept on cumming. I couldn't really count the ropes of cum, but it went on for a long time, with Kristen laughing and squealing as cum sprayed all over her face and tits.

"Damn!" she said when it was over.

"Get me something to clean myself up!" she demanded—of me, not Jim.

I went over to the towel rack, grabbed a hand towel, and

handed it to her. I felt shy now, wanting to cover up. My cock was soft and small. Jim's still hung down aggressively, still half-hard. It was hard to blame him. Kristen looked almost better in her sweaty animal state that she did all dolled up.

"I think ... I think I should go," I said. Ready to get out of here, resenting my kinky side and how it got me into so many emasculating situations.

"Okay," Kristen said, looking at me with kindness for the first time. As we locked eyes, I could see both her affection for me and the limits of that affection. It wasn't the true love I craved, far from it. But it was a look free of bullshit, and that meant a lot.

"I don't think he should leave just yet," Jim said, looking over at me with a different kind of look. As though he understood me better than I did myself.

Jim took Kristen's arm aggressively and guided her body to the ground. With intense aggression, he was on top of her.

"Spread your legs for me, bitch!" he said, totally in command again.

"No!" Kristen said. "No! I don't think Jason should see this."

"Oh, I think he should ... and you're gonna spread your slutty legs for this cock!"

Unable to help herself, she spread her legs wide. They were splayed out in both directions, feet poking into the sky.

Why hadn't she wanted me to see this?

There wasn't much gentleness to this fuck. Jim took a minute for her to get used to his fat mushroom head but then he was thrusting into her, hard.

"Oh yes!!" Kristen cried.

"Your pussy has some more cum for me, doesn't it?"

"Oh god yes!!" she screamed, so loud I instinctively looked around, but no one was anywhere near. She grabbed his ass, pulling him deeper inside. He was pushing in and out with intense power. I couldn't believe how far he could thrust inside her.

"Oh!" she kept calling as he hit bottom.

"Who's my slut?"

"I am!" she called out.

"Who's your slut that needs to cum?"

"I AM!!" she screamed again. "I'm your fucking slut!"

"Who owns this pussy?!" he called out as he slammed into her.

"Oh god, you do, Jim! ONLY YOU!!"

With that, I could see her body trembling and wracking underneath him, almost as if she were having a seizure. He was pushing her hands down and just letting her pussy spasm all over him. Only it wasn't just her pussy, it was a full body spasm.

I thought she was dying. Maybe a part of her was. "Oh fuuuuck!!" she cried out.

I realized I had cum again, stroking unconsciously to this amazing fuck. It almost hurt that time, but I was helpless not to. It was almost a dry cum; only a couple of drops came out.

After that orgasm, he stayed inside her. She casually wrapped her legs around his back, pushing him in and out slowly, making happy mewing noises almost like a cat.

It was then that I realized the scene had shifted. They were no longer fucking like animals whose bodies were perfect for each other. They were making love. She was kissing him, whispering to him. I thought I even heard her weeping.

I suddenly realized why she didn't want me there. Maybe because she knew that would hurt me more than all the small penis teasing.

I wrapped a towel around me and walked out. I thought I could hear her calling out to me. Maybe I was dreaming it or just irrationally hoping for something that couldn't be. I had to fight my own tears as I zipped up my pants and left. I thought about vowing never to see her again but I had been down that road before. I felt trapped.

Chapter 12

THE DAYS THAT FOLLOWED were as brutal as you would expect. I kept waiting for Kristen to call, hating that she didn't, knowing that I would eventually call her, and hating that she knew it.

The time with Kristen had damaged my sexual confidence even more. If she cared about me, then why had she done that? Whenever I met compelling girls my own age, my awareness of my own inadequacy ruled out any romantic approaches. *And yet Kristen had given me some of the best orgasms of my life.* Of that, there was no doubt. Didn't that count for something? If it hadn't been for her, my only orgasms during that time would have been by my own hand, nothing like the body draining ones she could pull out of me. *But should you spend your life chasing orgasms, or does that just make you an addict?*

A week went by, and still no call from her. On Saturday, I biked to the park and played ultimate Frisbee with my pals. I felt athletic, confident, a normal red blooded American male—free of my fetishes and insecurities. Out drinking after the game, I could feel the comfort in my own skin returning. The only problem was interacting with a few of the girls that were there. They were cute and hot and funny and smart. I could sense they wouldn't begin to understand or accept my desires. When they joked at chatted at me, it was like they were looking right through me. I couldn't figure out how to reclaim the cocky persona that would draw them to me.

Alone in my own bed, I felt my mind wander back to Kristen. The taboo and naughty things we had done. How much she had aroused me. The buttons she knew how to push. But more than that: *how she had put me in my sexual place.* And how much I had loved that. No, I didn't just love her interaction with me; it gave me relief, as if the charade of being someone else was over. *And yet I felt shattered inside.* If women arrived at romantic intimacy via sexual ecstasy, where did that leave me? Where did *she* leave me? What about building me up on the other side of tearing me down? What happened to that?

On Sunday, I knew I was going to call her. I could rationalize it by saying I was continuing my therapy, but I knew the truth: *I wanted to cum that hard again.* Well, and one other thing: I wanted to be seen and truly known—for all my inadequacies. If some humiliation was the price of not pretending around a girl, I would happily pay that price.

She was home when I called.

"I was waiting for your call," she said happily.

"I wasn't sure if I was going to call or not," I said, trying to sound more indifferent than I felt. My heart was pounding.

"Well, I'm glad you did … because I'm not quite done with you."

I didn't know how to take that.

"We're not finished with you yet … I put you through something pretty rough, but there's more to do."

"What?" I asked, filled with curiosity and dread.

"Well, I'll let that be a surprise … but I think you want to see this one through."

No hope restraining myself. Two days later, I was there. She was wearing an impossible little green sundress, one that she cut from a longer dress. The frayed edges lingered on her muscular thighs, as if her body was asking me if it was worthy. We both knew the answer to that.

I walked to the massage room, but she stopped me.

"Let's talk in the living room for a while," she said.

She saw my look.

"My roommate said she would be gone most of the day, and with the sun coming in, it feels good out here."

She sat across from me in a futon chair. I sat on the couch. The sun lit up her face. I couldn't help wondering if she was wearing anything under the sundress.

"So …" she said.

"So …"

"It was kind of a rough time for you when we last met up, I bet."

"Yeah."

"Sorry," she said. "I knew that would hurt, but there's a reason for it …"

I wasn't quite sure of the reason. All I knew was that I was desperately drawn to her and what she did for me.

She looked at me demandingly. It was amazing how easily she could shift from friendly affection to total control.

"What will you remember most?" she asked. "Be honest."

It took me a minute to answer, but then I said, "Watching you cum so hard. It was … beautiful."

"What else did you like?" she asked.

No more hesitating, I thought, *just brutal honesty*.

"I liked it when he took you from behind and made you scream and yell that you were a slut for his cock."

"Oh you liked that, huh?" she smiled, but in a stern way, expecting me to treat her secrets as such.

"Yeah."

"You like talking about it with me now, don't you?" she asked.

"Yeah."

"Here's what I want to do, Jason," she said. "I want to take your little dick out now and stroke it while you tell me all about what you saw."

"But your roommate …"

"Well, she shouldn't be back anytime soon. And if she does come in, well, you need to be free enough to let it happen, let whatever it is happen. No more shame."

I was beyond obedience at this point. I was either chasing my fetish or chasing the truth, tomorrow be damned either way. I reached inside, pulled my already hard dick out, and started stroking.

"That's it," she said, "but I don't want you to cum right away. Stroke it, bring yourself to the edge, stroke a bit slower. But don't cum." After watching me follow her instructions, she said, "Yes, good. Now, tell me all about what you saw."

And I did. As I stroked, I told her what it was like to watch her fuck. How intense it was to watch. What it was like to see her cum that hard, her whole body shaking. Especially since I had failed to make her feel the same way. I didn't tell her how much it hurt. That was the one part I kept to myself and maybe the one part she didn't need to be told.

Each time I was close to cumming, I would hold back, releasing the tension while she guided me through it. My balls and cock ached from not cumming, but I held on.

She could tell I was close. She got up and sat down next to me.

We both had our legs up on the table. I could feel the scrape of stubble on her brown calves. I almost shot just from that sensation. She moved my hands off my cock. It was standing straight up, red and hard and dripping with precum.

"So, you did good. You held out for a really long time."

"Yeah, maybe for not much longer."

"That's okay," she said. "You need to be able to hold out. This will help you in some sexual situations. I want you to keep practicing, keep going right on the edge and coming back."

"Okay," I said.

"This is different than jacking off at home. The desire to cum is way more intense, right? With me watching, I mean." She looked at my wickedly and down at my cock as well. I almost shot again.

"Yes."

"That's right," she said. "It's like it would be in a real sexual situation. And, inside a sexy woman's pussy, you don't want to squirt right away, now do you?"

"No."

"Are you ready to cum now? Shall I release you?"

"Yes!" I said, ashamed of my eagerness. I could tell from her quick smile how pleased she was. Yeah, she pretty much owned me. After all the indignities, somehow I trusted her. *Because she's the only woman who has been one hundred percent honest with you …*

She wrapped her hand around my dick, squeezing it softly.

"Ohhhhhh!" I exhaled.

"So you understand now, right?" she said.

"Yes," I said.

"You understand why my pussy needs a big cock, right?"

"Yeah …"

"It's not because I'm loose down there. You've had your fingers in, and you know it's plenty tight."

"Yes …"

"Why is it then?"

"Because I'm too small," I said. *It felt so right to say it.*

"Yes, that's right, you're too small … too small for what?"

"For filling up a girl's pussy," I confessed.

"That's true. But it's more than that," she said.

"I'm too small to make a pussy cum … hard," I said.

She took her hand off my cock for a moment, likely sensing I was about to squirt all over her if she didn't.

"Yes, but there's more," she said. "This part isn't going to be easy for you. You're really too small to fuck at all." She almost blurted it out. I could tell she didn't want to say it, despite her love of the truth.

"I am?" I asked.

"Yeah, you are," she said. "Well, except for virgins or abnormally tight girls."

I was so close to cumming.

"Or maybe girls who are totally in love with you, before the love settles in."

I wanted to protest. Somehow her words didn't seem right, and I know they didn't seem fair. But then my life experience to this point could not contradict her.

"You have a lot to offer a girl, you know that, right?"

"Yeah."

"Just not fucking."

"No, not fucking."

"So you need to find other ways, right? To please a girl."

"Yes," I admitted. Such a relief to admit it.

"And I'm going to help you with that," she said, stroking me calmly again.

"Okay."

"But first, I think that little dick deserves to cum. Does it feel good?"

"Yes!"

"How good?"

"It feels amazing!" I said. I was going to explode soon.

"You know why?"

"Why?"

"Because I own that little cock."

Ohh ...

"How does it feel to know?"

"*Know*?" I asked.

"That your cock can't make my pussy cum, but I can make you squirt whenever I want."

"Ohhhhh ..."

"Whenever I want!" she insisted, stroking harder, easily

grasping me with a few fingers. Then she proved she *could* read my mind. "And it only takes a few fingers! Let me see that little dick squirt." She was stroking me super-fast. "NOW!!"

I squirted on command, spasming into the air, rocketing a few spurts up to my face and neck.

"That's it!" she said. "That's a good little dick!"

I bucked my hips up. The combination of her teasing and stimulation was way too much.

"Nice," she said. "You really did cum hard, huh?"

"Yeah," I said.

"See, for you, with a small cock like that, a teasing hand job is one of the best orgasms you can have."

I couldn't argue.

"It's a lot tighter around you than a pussy would be."

True.

"Now, go get cleaned up, but don't get dressed, and meet me in the massage room."

I did. I was still in obedience mode, feeling great from the cum. I wondered when my "The heck with her!" protest mode would return. I went to the restroom, washed and scrubbed off.

When I opened the massage room door, the first thing I saw was her yellow sundress hanging from a towel rack. Then I saw her, *totally nude on the table*.

"Come over here," she said, before I could really think straight.

I walked over next to her, totally in her command.

"Now I want you to put your hand in my pussy," she said. "I want you to feel how wet it is."

I put my fingers down inside her, admiring her perfection as her breasts and hips swayed to my touch. It was true; she was really wet.

"Remember that feeling," she said. "That's what a pussy feels like when it's really turned on."

"How did you get so turned on?"

"Well, taking control over you, it got me wet. And then thinking about how badly I needed to be fucked."

No hesitation. I took advantage of the situation, moving my fingers in and out of her pussy as she grabbed a breast in each hand, as if she imagined her lover grabbing her roughly while he fucked her deeply.

"Now it's time for some lessons for you, some lessons that will help you."

Lessons? I was just happy to be moving my fingers in and out of her.

"Look at me. You see that I'm ready to be fucked, right?"

It was true. She was squirming on the mat. I was surprised she hadn't fallen off. Her pussy was dripping all over my hand.

"You probably want to fuck me right now, don't you?"

"Yes," I said.

"But you realize the problem, now, don't you?"

"Yes."

"I need a deep, crazy-hard fucking, and you don't have the equipment for it—simple as that."

"I know."

"When I'm bucking all over the place like this, I need an animal pounding, and you're not going to be able to keep it in me."

"I know!" I said, a little forcefully.

She smiled with satisfaction, pleased at how quickly I had acknowledged the truth of what she said.

"Exactly! If you put your tiny dick inside me now, we both know what would happen. It would tickle more than it would satisfy."

"Yeah," I said, relieved to be admitting the truth.

"So here's what you need to do," she said. "If you get a girl in this situation, where she's dripping and hot like I am, don't put your little dick inside her."

"Okay."

"Trying to fuck her when you know you can't … will just take her out of the mood."

"So should I try a toy?"

"No!" she said. "I know it seems like a big toy would be the best thing, but it usually isn't."

"Why?" I said, continuing to move my fingers in and out while she talked and moaned.

"Because toys … well, they just aren't like the real thing."

"Okay."

"Sometimes they work, but big dildos aren't really what girls buy at sex shops. They buy little buzzing vibrators. That's why, with a cock of your size, you need to focus on clit orgasms."

"Okay."

"It's not the same as a deep vaginal orgasm, or that clit-vaginal double feature a big thick cock can pull out of you,"—Kristen seemed to be losing the point for a second, but she soon came back to reality—"but it's still pretty awesome, and some girls don't know any other kind."

Kristen proceeded to spend the next hour showing me how to work her clit with my hand, and then my tongue. She told me I had a natural talent for oral sex. She taught me how to rotate my tongue around the clit, backing off when she got too close.

"Your technique could be better, but that's due to your lack of experience." She smiled, and my cock twitched. "You do have that passion," she added. "You really go for it, like you love being down there. And that makes up for a lot."

But while I did Okay with my tongue, I did even better with my hand. And to be honest, I liked it better. I could really see her that way, see her squirming all over. I seemed to have a knack for knowing just when she needed more direct stimulation on her clit and when to pull away and rub the whole area, increasing the tempo to work with her own rhythm. I knew when to apply more pressure with the fingers. And I could see my hand had a huge advantage over my dick. I could stretch open her entrance or add as many fingers as I needed to get a reaction. I was really working her!

Before I knew it, she was clutching my hand between her legs, squeezing and cumming. It wasn't as intense as the body-shaking orgasms I saw her have a week ago, but it wasn't shabby either. She called out "I'm cumming!" several times in a way that was gratifying.

I was still jealous I couldn't just pound her into submission with her legs wrapped desperately around me, but making her cum so good still did wonders for my ego.

"Damn!" she said. "Your pussy-eating skills are decent, but your hand ... your hand is brilliant. So this is what you need to do with girls." Kristen was casually stroking her pussy. "The first time you get them undressed, you need to make them cum like that. Before you try to put your little dick inside them, before you try to cum yourself. Got that?" she demanded.

"Got it." I was starting to feel better about myself already. I could still be confident of making a woman feel awesome ... if I knew my limitations and worked at what I *could* do.

"For many girls, they won't need anything more from you," she said. "So when you fuck them, even it isn't the best fuck ever, they are already satisfied."

"Got it." This was making sense.

"And they know you are attentive to them and put their needs first. Whereas, if you try to put your little dick inside them first, you're likely to squirt really fast, right?"

"Right," I reluctantly admitted.

"And either way, they will think you are selfish, putting your needs ahead of theirs."

"What about you?" I asked. "Are you completely satisfied?"

I was scared to hear this particular answer. But I needed to. I had to.

She put her fingers back inside her pussy, as if she was doing a quick gut check.

"To be honest, yeah," she said. "Of course, if you had a big thick cock it would be inside me right now, and that first big orgasm would have been the warm-up, but … I'm good."

I smiled.

"And," she went on, "I appreciate not having to pretend that I'm obligated to fuck your tiny cock."

I didn't smile so much at that piece of ruthlessness, but I could see what she was getting at.

"In my case, an orgasm like this, it sets me up to have a really good day," she said. "It's as if I had woken up and masturbated, but about five times more intense having someone else do it."

I did smile at that.

"Okay," Kristen said. "That was enough for today. Can you come back next week? We still have a little more to go."

Next week would not be a problem. For the first time, I was beginning to see a crack of light in the "break you down/build you back up" plan.

I began to carry myself a bit different around attractive women. I felt … more confident again. But in a deeper way. Like I had a confidence that couldn't be exposed. Even if I had to take my pants off. The shame and dread seemed to have faded in favor of a quiet kind of flow. I even had a woman ask me out on a pinball date. It wasn't a romantic date, but I couldn't help but think my relaxed style was part of the reason. I found myself looking forward to the next week with Kristen … and not just to the orgasm.

Chapter 13

⎯

THE NEXT WEEK, KRISTEN greeted me at the door wearing a more professional outfit—a dressy skirt and jacket with heels. Her hair was pulled back, and she even had black glasses on, a sort of librarian fantasy. But the athleticism of her body made the outfit seem like a sexy contrast. Animal power and brains. I felt weak.

She led me into the living room.

"So, you like my outfit today?"

"Yeah."

"I thought you might. It's the kind of thing a girlfriend of yours might wear. You might see her like that as she comes home from work."

She sat down in a chair and pointed toward the couch across from her.

"At first it's hot to think about all the guys that must hit on her, because you're feeling secure in the relationship," Kristen laid it out, "but then, something shifts. You see that she is not paying as much attention to you after work. She isn't in the mood for sex as often. She goes out more with her friends."

I wasn't sure where Kristen was going with this.

"Her indifference probably turns you on, just like me sitting over here, beyond your sexual reach."

Ugh. Twitch.

"But you also know you're losing her, that she's drifting away. So … what do you do?

"I take her on a special night out," I said. "Give her a chance to tell me if anything's wrong."

"And what else?" Kristen asked.

"After dinner, I take her out dancing."

"Okay, that's a good start," Kristen said. "But what about when you get her home? Do you try to fuck her?"

"Not right off the bat. I focus on tender lovemaking, giving her great oral sex."

"Not bad," Kristen said. "I've taught you well. But there's one more thing you need to do."

"What's that?"

"Let her in on your fantasies … all of them."

"Okay."

"And you know what that means, don't you?"

"I think so."

"It means telling her you fantasize about her with other guys."

Even hearing her say it, it was a little bit hard, and not in a sexually arousing way.

"So, do I bring up the fantasies right away?"

"No," Kristen said. "At first you focus on the best sex you can give her. You never want to impose your fetishes on a girl. But at the first sign of problems, at the first sign she is bored sexually, start bringing up the fantasies … and ask about hers."

"Okay."

"You'll want to have a couple of toys handy, like a big fleshy dildo, so you can share with her what you want, and see her reaction."

"Okay."

"So here's the bad news, Jason," she said. "This is the last time we are going to play together … for a while."

I'm sure I looked disappointed. Maybe relieved, but also disappointed.

"You've learned a lot, and there's more to do, but it doesn't involve me."

I was quiet. I had a sinking feeling she didn't mean *a while*. She meant forever.

"The thing is, you need to get out there, get some confidence with other girls."

I felt bad, but somehow it felt right too. I could finally admit it to myself: the relationship was too unequal.

"I'm going to give you some homework, some things to work on."

"What are those?" I asked.

"Well, it's a fourteen point plan."

"A what?"

She handed me a piece of paper.

"Go ahead and read it."

She had titled the piece, "Sexual Success for the Small Penis Man." It was funny to see all this written out in her masculine, jagged scrawl. Penmanship was not her subject.

The instructions were numbered, just as she said.

"Read it to me," she said, putting her beautiful hose-encased legs next to mine.

So I did:

1. Do everything you can to improve your overall sexual skills, including oral sex, finger sex, nipple caressing, sensual massage, and teaching yourself to last longer before you cum.

2. Do not let your inadequacies affect you outside the bedroom. Become as successful as possible in your field, including financially. Stay physically fit.

3. Work on your emotional and intimate relationship skills. Always remain humble and try to be the best partner you can be.

4. Work on being naturally assertive so that you are not seen as a nice guy who can be pushed around or exploited.

5. Cultivate a bit of wild side outside of work. Pursue creative passions, keep an edge to your personality.

6. Focus your sexual energy less on women and more on accomplishing things that give you an authentic sense of power and status.

7. Remember to stay true to your own integrity. Use your power to raise others up. That kind of power makes women swoon.

8. Never let your manhood outside of the bedroom be defined by your smallness inside of it. Be a strong, brave man who has a reputation for looking out for those you love.

9. Never, ever, try to pretend to girls that you can make them feel the way a true alpha stud can make them feel. Know and respect your sexual place, but remember you can still make a girl feel VERY good.

10. Don't impose your cuckold and submissive fantasies on a girl. When you're first dating, focus on making her happy and don't draw attention to any submissive fantasies until she brings them up. Don't forget anal sex, which can be a great option for a smaller guy if she is into it. Perhaps when she is drunk.

We both laughed out loud at the way that last line came out. Years later I would remember it as vintage Kristen.

11. The second you sense there is a problem satisfying

your girlfriend, whether it's the first date or the tenth, you MUST start dropping hints that you are open to fantasies, role playing, and open discussions about any sexual topics that turn her on. Be ready. Even when she seems totally in love with you, be ready.

12. Remember that being painfully honest and open when the sex gets stale, as it often will if you are under-endowed, is very important to avoid cheating and deception.

13. If by some chance you do meet a girl who is perfectly fulfilled by you, despite your size, you may still have to eventually bring up your size inadequacy feelings and cuckold fantasies in order to tap into your own desires.

14. Many attractive women are not fully aware of how vulnerable they are to cheating on their mates until they are unexpectedly seduced. You must prepare her for this possibility even if she is resistant or if it is hard to talk about. This will plant the seed that she can bring you into the fantasy (or reality) instead of cheating on you.

15. Don't make her feel slutty and ashamed if she admits to being unsatisfied or even having cheated on you. Let her know that getting deeply fucked by a real man is a primal need for most women, and she has nothing to be ashamed of for craving total submission and ECSTASY, just as you have nothing to be ashamed of for not being able to do that to her. These needs have nothing to do with her love for you or fidelity. Like it or not, they are deeper than love. Be able to talk about them openly in fantasy, but don't assume you will need to make them a reality. At the same time, be prepared to make them a reality if that is what's necessary.

I put the paper down. It was a lot to absorb. That last point was the doozy. It was not easy to read, but I could tell she was right. *With all the experiences we had shared ... all the points hit home.*

"Do you understand?" Kristen asked me.

She smiled. She could tell I was aroused by reading the list, but didn't seem to let on, other than crossing and uncrossing her legs to give me a sense of how her power skirt clung to her body.

"What we're really talking about is small penis acceptance, but not shame," Kristen said. "You get that, right?"

"I got it."

"Most of the guys I know with small dicks are insecure in the bedroom and assholes outside of it, trying to prove something," she said. "I'm giving you a totally different road. You understand?"

"Yeah," I said. She seemed to know where this was going and that it was turning me on, too. She always knew.

"A lot of big guys, they just get cocky with it, and it gets old—inside and outside of bed," Kristen said. "That's where you can work it. Work your ass off to be a better man. And in most ways, you can be."

For some reason, this honest conversation about my sexual liabilities and what I could do about them was really turning me on. Kristen seemed a little flushed in the face as well. I realized later she must have truly enjoyed having this kind of brute naked power over me, without any pretense.

"So, are you ready for your final lesson?" she said, putting a knowing hand on my erect dick under my pants.

"Yeah," I said, wondering what was in store for me.

"C'mon," she beckoned to me. But instead of leading me to the massage room, she led me to her bedroom—that bedroom I had fantasized about so often. She stopped me outside the door.

"Let's pretend you're my co-worker, and my husband is out

of town. I asked you to come over to help me with a deadline, but you could tell from the beginning something was up. The sexual tension has been building between us for a while. A tour of the house ends outside the bedroom. I couldn't be more obvious …"

She put her arms around me, kissed me once on the lips.

With a confidence that surprised me, I not only kissed her back, but placed my hands on her ass and pulled her closer.

"Ahhhh," she said, smiling at me with surprised delight. "You know what I want?" She kissed me once more. "I wanna fuck." She moved her hips against my crotch, rotating in a sensual manner. Damn she was a goddess.

She grabbed my hand and pulled me into the bedroom. I was worried that I was falling into another humiliation trap. She had taught me how to please her, but I knew all too well what would happen if I tried to fuck her.

She pulled off her sundress in one fluid motion, tossing it on the floor. I stared at her intimidating body with lust, she looked a bit like some pictures of a young pop diva I used to jack off to when she was younger but beginning to flesh out her hips.

"Can you give me one of those massages you were telling me about?" she asked.

Realizing she was still role playing, I said, "Sure, let's get you down on the bed." I guided her down and laid her on her stomach. Kneeling on top of her, still fully clothed myself, I worked on the massage moves she had taught me, starting with the more neutral parts of her body, neck, and shoulders. Working my way down to her back. But before I got to her ass, I started again on her feet.

"Ohhhh," she moaned as I pulled away. "You're teasing me." *It's about time you got some of that*, I thought to myself as I worked her toes and calf muscles. Working my way up to her thighs, I could feel her trembling anticipation. I almost whipped off my pants and stuffed my cock inside her, but I knew better. I knew I had to pace myself. I kneaded her sexy leg muscles and hinted at going farther up her thigh, but always pulled back.

She started pushing her ass up in response, clearly wanting my fingers to move up farther … up into her. And the more I withheld, the more she moaned.

Finally I shoved three fingers directly inside her—hoping that was enough to make an impression but not enough to cause pain.

"Oh my God!" she said. "Oh!!"

It was great to feel her squirming, almost trying to get away from my hand as I pulled her closer. For perhaps the first time ever, she was in *my* rhythm. Without missing a beat, I flipped her over onto her back and moved up against her, working my fingers in and out of her. In this position, I could get at her clit a lot more easily, so I worked it.

She spread her legs for me wantonly wide, and I worked my fingers in and out, bringing friction to her clit here and there but pacing it all, savoring the moment.

"Damn that feels so good!!"

"You're damn right it does!" I said, taking control. "Guess what I'm gonna do next?" I asked her.

"What?" she asked, squirming on my hand, looking at me helplessly.

"I'm gonna make that pussy cum!"

"Oh my god I want to fuck!!" she said, rubbing her clit while clenching her hand between her legs.

She quickly rolled off the side of the bed and walked over to her dresser. She grabbed what looked to be a large clear dildo, with some kind of strap.

She kneeled before me, unzipping me. Without breaking character, she took the plastic dildo and slipped it over my cock. Just her grip on my cock made me strain hard.

"Oh wow your cock is really big!!" she said, looking at me with lust as she worked to secure the straps on my back.

It was amazing to watch a big thick cock dangling from my body, almost hard.

"My husband can't please me," she looked up at me expectantly. "God I need this!!!"

I reached down and grabbed the clear soft plastic "cock" with my right hand, moving it up and down. It was amazing to feel the heaviness and extent of the thing in my hands. You could see my own cock a little more than halfway up the sleeve, with extra room around it. But she pretended it was all mine.

"Oh yeah!" she said. "I can't wait to fuck that big cock!" She lay back on her bed and spread her legs wide again, moving her hands up her thighs. "C'mon, get it in there!"

Remembering her advice, I kneeled in front of her, but I stopped deferring to her. I pushed her legs even farther apart and immediately began working the large head of the dildo into her pussy.

"Oh wow!" she said. "Be careful, I'm not used to such a big cock. My husband has a really tiny penis."

I was totally erect with this smack talk and the different position she had cleverly put me in. I pushed the dildo in about halfway and heard another gasp from Kristen.

"Take your time," she pleaded, "Let me get used to it."

I started working it back and forth inside her. The movement was a little awkward—I was getting used to the tug of the straps from behind me—but it did seem to come pretty naturally. It took focus, but I was able to start thrusting inside her faster.

"Daaammn," she said. "That feels gooood."

Thrusting into her was a weird experience. I couldn't feel much sensation on my cock inside the sleeve, but I was rock hard. It was amazing to savor the pressure of the plastic cock up inside her. The in and out friction was like nothing I had experienced, and the resistance from her pussy on each thrust from being so filled up was just as novel. I felt a flash of jealousy for guys with cocks big enough to feel that kind of pressure all the time, and the way she seemed to work in rhythm with that pressure. Enough!

I pushed her hands back while she fought with me in fake resistance, then I pushed the cock all the way into her.

"Aaaaaah!" she said. I was so deep inside her. I started moving in and out in long strokes, pushing all the way into her each time.

"Fuck!" she said. "Fuck me!"

I kept on pushing. As I pulled in and out, I looked down to watch her pussy stretched wide around the dildo. I was able to push in pretty hard without losing the rhythm.

Then I had an inspiration.

"Does this feel better than your husband's little dick?"

"Oh god! So much better!" she said. "Fuck!" she cried out for emphasis, as she started to rub her clit feverishly. "Keep going like that!"

I was able to thrust in and out pretty quickly, not slamming her but with enough force. I could feel her pussy contract in rhythm along with me, a swelling sensation. I suddenly realized what that meant: she was going to cum all over me.

"I just knew you'd know how to fuck me!!!" she cried out, pulling me in as hard as she could. The base of the dildo was jammed all the way in, and I could feel her tremors beginning.

"Oh yeah," I said, all cocky now. "Cum for me like a good little slut!"

I could feel her body tense up and then spasm in release. "Cummmming!" she said.

She pushed the cock out of her pussy with the force of her orgasm as her legs spasmed.

It wasn't the extreme kind of cum I had seen her experience at the gym, but it was a way harder cum than anything I had managed with my naked cock or even my hand in the past.

"Daaammmn …" she said.

I was amazed I hadn't cum myself, not from the sensations

but from the power rush, that I had ripped an orgasm out of her.

"I needed that cum so bad!" Kristen said. I wasn't sure if she was still role-playing or not, but I did know she had cum.

I lay down next to her, happy that I had made her orgasm, happy that I had taken control of the situation.

"You were great," she said, reaching over and grabbing my plastic dildo cock, which was sticking up in the air, perpetually ready.

"That's a nice big cock you have," she said.

"Why, thank you!" I said. We both laughed.

"So," she said, "you see what I'm getting at, right?"

"I think so," I said. "You want me to ... to always be ready, always have the confidence to take control of a woman's body when I have to."

"That's right!" she said. "And make sure to keep the toys around in case you need them. Just don't get dildos that are too big. You see how this dildo is big, but not huge?"

"Yeah," I said as she stroked it.

"That's because toys are harder to take than real cocks," she said. "My favorite real cocks are around eight inches. My favorite toys are about this size."

"Which is?"

"Seven inches, pretty thick," she said. "This is a good size for a strap-on toy for you. You can get it all the way inside most girls and push hard, but it's still waaaay bigger than your little dick, see?" She continued to casually stroke the plastic cock.

"Yeah," I said. She laughed. It was true. My cock was only a small part of that bigger plastic toy. You'd have to grow my cock several times over to get to the outer edges of the plastic.

"Of course, the only problem is that you won't be able to feel much when you're fucking a girl with this strap-on," she said.

"Right," I said.

"But that's fair, because she won't feel much when you're NOT using the toy, will she?"

"No," I admitted. Kristen smiled.

"And why is that?" she asked me sternly.

"Because my cock is too small to fill up a pussy," I said without hesitating.

"Yes!" Kristen smiled with satisfaction. "But that doesn't mean you can't have loads of fun in the bedroom." Her hand relaxed around the dildo. I found myself wishing she would grip it hard.

"So if I have a toy, does that mean that I ... have enough for a girl?" I asked, looking over at her.

"Honestly?" she said.

"When have you not been?" I asked.

"Well, it's a mixed bag," she said. "Most guys think girls want a huge dildo, but if you can get them to try a toy, this size is really better. This bigger cock will make most girls feel really good, but it may awaken them further to the real thing ... and to your shortcomings as far as penetration goes. They might start thinking, *If this bigger toy cock feels so much better ...*"

I finished the thought for her. "... *Then how good would a real big one feel?*"

"Exactly," Kristen said. "And it's not quite the same, the toy. Some of the physical sensations are similar, but ..."

Once again I finished the sentence for her. "Not the psychological feeling of being totally taken."

"Exactly!" she said. I had almost surprised myself.

"And you could see. It was a good cum, but it wasn't ...

"A mind-blowing one," I said.

"Yeah," she said, "and there are other things about big cocks ... like the ones that are big squirters. And pulling down a guy's pants and seeing a big pussy-killing cock flop out, it's just so intense ... It's just ..." She sighed and rubbed herself a bit. "You just have to be open to wherever a relationship takes you." She paused. "But just don't forget," she added, "girls love a great fuck, and a part of you needs to be put in your place. You need to figure out how to be both dominant and submissive. I should have called that point number sixteen, now that I think of it!"

"Hmmmm," I said, contemplating my situation. I needed some time alone to process all this, but I didn't feel depressed like I had in the past after our sessions. Something had shifted.

"Ready for one more cum?" she said.

She started gripping the plastic cock tighter as she stroked.

"Let's make that little dick squirt inside here!" she said, stroking me faster.

I knew it wouldn't take long. It felt so good with her gripping the dildo tight like that.

"Oh yeah!" she said. "Look at your tiny cock twitching inside here." She worked it up and down. "Don't you wish you had a cock this big?"

"Oh god, yeah!" I said.

"And to think, if you had a cock like this dildo, you'd be the smallest lover I've had in years," she said, smiling wickedly at me and gripping the plastic hard around my cock. "C'mon, let me see that tiny dick squirt in there!!"

That was all I could take. I started squirting into the dildo, bucking my hips off of the bed.

"Oh GOD!!" I said.

"That's it," she said with a smug smile.

I was spent. I cleaned up in her bathroom while she got dressed.

In the living room, she was waiting for me. She had cleaned the dildo and put it in a bag for me.

"That's for you to keep," she said. "And use!!" She gave me her best teasing smile. "I'm really proud of you." Wrapping her arms around me, she added, "Now go get yourself some more of this." She kissed me sensuously on the lips.

I grabbed her ass one more time.

"Hey!" she said, looking at me disapprovingly.

But I could tell she was impressed.

I have not seen Kristen since.

Chapter 14

⌒

THE NEXT FEW YEARS of my dating life were pretty darn good. My size insecurities didn't plague me anymore. That probably sounds strange to you. But I just seemed to have a clear view of who I was. What I brought to the table, and what I lacked, only without the judgment.

Yeah, I missed Kristen sometimes. This is what bothered me most: for every time I was sad, there were ten times when I missed our kinky games. Even though I knew those games were fleeting. Even though I knew deep down she didn't love me. She loved me, but with a lower case "l." Even if you've struggled to find love as much as I have, you sure as heck know the difference between the two. But yeah, I missed her. On the other hand, leaning forward into your life is not so bad either. And whatever Kristen's failings, that's where she came through.

Asking girls out was a lot easier after Kristen. Enough of them said yes to make my life pretty interesting. One girl I dated—a medical technician who was used to being in charge—actually said, "I love how you made me your slut!" after I had brought her to countless orgasms with my tongue, fingers, and then with her vibrator. Without asking for her permission to make her cum. *Just, you know, taking it.* In a way she completely and happily allowed, just like I had seen those big dicked alpha guys do.

It turns out I was pretty good at playing an alpha male type role for certain girls. There was a fitness instructor who loved being tied down by someone stronger. No mean stuff, just restraint, then plenty of orgasms while she was living out that feeling of helplessness. Fortunately I had lifted enough weights after Kristen kicked me in the ass that I was pretty strong. I could tell that made a difference to Tina, my fitness instructor girlfriend.

The fact I could hold her down even when she offered serious resistance was a big turn-on to her. I could tell that if I hadn't been strong enough, she would have been turned off. But I was, and so was she. I was pretty good at understanding what made girls tick after all. I suppose the fact that I could afford to take them out to nice dinners and buy thoughtful gifts for them didn't hurt either.

So that was my late twenties—dating girls, not sure what I was looking for exactly, but enjoying my newfound ability to reel them in. The only real glitch was one woman, Nadine. Nadine was a black belt in karate, and while I was a bit stronger than her, she was not at all intimidated by me physically. We only tried to fool around once, and when she got me undressed and my cock hard, I could tell she was disappointed. I pretended not to notice and even dialed it up a notch.

I did my oral thing on her instead and she was happy enough, but I could tell she wanted to be dominated and in this case, I didn't feel like I had the touch she needed. We went our separate ways with no hard feelings. I put that experience behind me and hit the dating scene again. But deep down I realized there were some women my newfound confidence couldn't reach. Trouble is, those were typically the girls I wanted most.

The downside of my newfound confidence was that I

wasn't always fulfilled. Either I found myself in what I now call "vanilla" relationships where my taboo fantasies were not welcome, or else I was living out the girls' fantasies without doing justice to my own. Maybe that's why none of these late twenties girlfriends have lasted. I could see that at some point, one of them could become more serious. But what was I looking for? What was holding me back?

Maybe it was me. I could play that alpha role, but there was something missing. I felt like a fraud, waiting for a girl like Nadine to see right through me and call me out. *No, it was way more serious than that. I wanted to be called out. I needed to be called out.* In the back of my mind, I found myself wondering … wondering about how I felt so much closer to my sexual destiny playing kinky games with Kristen than I had since. In some bizarre way, that felt more normal to me, more right, than anything that followed.

But then … things changed again. And in a very, very big way.

Chapter 15

FAST FORWARD THREE MORE years, and now you're practically reading this as a type. I'm thirty-two.

I'm sure you'll be surprised to know that as I type, Beth is in the next room, sleeping on the bed. Yes, that's right. *Beth from high school*. We're together. Not only that, but we're married. Before you start to choke on this fairy tale ending, let me throw a bit of cold water on it. This is Beth's second marriage. She has a goatee-sporting pain in the ass of an ex-husband we both have to deal with now. I don't know if I should be happy or pissed that he is such a bad parent. He only takes Beth's daughter Allie twice a month. Allie is four years old now, old enough to feel the sting of her father's absence. I try to pick up the slack but Allie has yet to call me "Dad," nor would I want her to. She is finally comfortable letting me walk her to the bus stop when Beth has to work early.

You may wonder how I managed to get Beth to fall in love with me, and if I did, why I'm writing this book. Well, the falling in love part I owe to Kristen. Kristen sparked me into trying to excel in my life. She scared the shit out of me, in a very good way. She made me realize that I needed a triumph.

Call it over-compensation if you want. I prefer to think of it as a fierce push toward excellence.

I needed to work on my skills, not only in the bedroom but in life. By the time I ran into Beth again, I was not only a teacher but a published author on urban school planning. I was not a gym rat anymore, but I still stayed in shape. And it didn't hurt that Allie took to me immediately. I wasn't rich, but I had moved on from the public schools and taken more lucrative private school positions. I managed to bank the difference and I was in a pretty good position financially. On some level I must have realized that in my case, to be considered "husband material", I needed to have my financial shit together. I suppose it didn't hurt that Beth was coming off a marriage of emotional deprivation. There are different ways the sexual spark can be extinguished—emotional neglect is one I had not considered. Beth's ex-husband was great at getting women into bed but not as good at keeping them. Of course, I had the opposite problem.

Beth and I met at one of my speaking gigs - in New York City of all places. She surprised me afterward and was clearly impressed by what I had accomplished since I left her house in shame almost fifteen years earlier. I think maybe that determination not to be defined by my shortcomings was what turned her on the most. I took the judgment she and her sister placed on me, and on some fundamental level, I had not let it define me.

I suppose there was some luck involved too maybe there always is; I had only recently moved to Boston and she was only two hours away in Hartford. Two hours might not have been viable for a new relationship, but with our history, it was nothing for me to drive down and see her every few Fridays. The dates added up.

I know it probably sounds odd that she would be so attracted to me after our prior misadventures. All I can tell you is that we had both changed. If I had evolved, she had softened. I guess she you could say she had been humbled by her own difficulties. But if I had to pick one thing, it was probably seeing me speak in front of a audience, working the room with authority and showing absolutely no sign of the self-esteem crisis she had inflicted for better and for worse. And yeah, I knew how to take care of her. Fuck it; we loved each other, simple as that, and no stopping it either. Timing is everything. I'll grant you that, but six months of dating was all it took.

And no, I didn't hold back on the sex. On our third date, things got hot and heavy and I made my move.

"God damn, you know how to eat a pussy!" was a line that told me I might just have a chance with Beth the second time around.

I didn't ask her how I compared with her former lovers and no, we never talked about our adolescent incidents. I brought it up once in the interest of brutal honesty, and she said, "Jason, I was young then. I was young." Then she wrapped her brown arms around me and kissed me into another place.

We were married at the grand old age of thirty-one. By then I had ditched my bachelor pad in Boston and we had bought in on a new place in suburban Connecticut. It wasn't a big wedding but that didn't matter one iota. She was the girl of my dreams and I would have married her in a garage. As it was, we married at the foot of Pike's Peak in Colorado Springs. When she read her own vows, she started trembling so much that her friend Kim had to hold her steady. It was hard for me to fathom how she could love me that much.

To be honest I've never felt worthy of that kind of love. As much as I've fought for a better life, a part of me feels like I don't deserve it. Like I wouldn't mind jumping over the ledge to remind myself about the darkness. The darkness I'm afraid I'll always be drawn to. I'll always wonder if that isn't the purpose of these nastier sex dreams. To cover the darkness up. To orgasm me into numbness, or into the next day.

But then I am a married man and I can afford a few idle

thoughts after a long day. And on the good days, the snoring brown goddess you're lucky to call your wife has her arms wrapped almost too tight around you. Those nights you sleep like a pardoned criminal. And the questions can wait.

But when I turned thirty-two, I found myself typing this story. I don't know what started the outpouring. I guess it was when I noticed Beth and I weren't having sex every night anymore. The passion was still there, but she wasn't ripping my clothes off when I got home from work either. I'm not sure these are the right fires to stoke, but burn they do. And so I write.

It was about this time she started travelling more for work. There was a legitimate reason. Her company was opening a new office in Philadelphia and she was needed for corporate training. It was too far away for her to come home all the time, though she tried to get back whenever she could, because Allie wasn't comfortable staying with me alone for more than a couple of nights.. I wasn't the only one who slept better when Beth was around.

I could have sworn that after one of Beth's trips, she had a happy smile on her face that seemed to imply a deep sexual satisfaction. I had not seen that look on a girl's face in a long time; I felt my gut churning. I resisted the urge to check Beth's email or go through her purse.

That's when I had to admit it: I haven't been one hundred percent honest with Beth. She had written off our youthful misadventures as just that. Whereas for me, those brutal erotics had worked their way into the core of my sexual identity. Winning my dream girl's heart got in the way of a lesson I had already learned: don't hold your secrets back.

I had realized my dream, and somehow that dream felt far more important than my fetishes. Not to mention being a different kind of father to Allie, in my own way. A way that would have its ups and downs, but still … I could sense a different kind of joy building. Beth could see it too, like the day she blurted out: "You're going to make a seriously great father!" after watching me patiently teaching Allie how to tie her Angry Birds shoelaces through her indignant tears.

Also: I trusted Beth. Trusted her one hundred percent. I knew deep down she would never cheat on me, ever. Despite how Kristen warned me. A part of me wanted her to cheat. Heck, I even hoped she had, as terrible as that sounds. But I didn't speak of it. Things were still too good. We didn't have that daily passion, but a couple times a week we found a way to have some fun. And I always made her cum, of that there was no question. Beyond the sex was the closeness. We were always good to each other. I never felt her withholding. If anything I was the one with secrets.

And yet ... the doubt. Or was it a fetish, something I could never shake? The thing is, I only wanted it to happen if she did. If Beth was with another man only to get me off, it wouldn't do a thing for me. But if one day she woke up, realized she was sexually famished, went out and got her brains fucked out—well there was nothing I craved more. That craving was becoming so intense I couldn't think of it in terms of good or bad. It felt like fate. The cruel, intense perfection of it made my knees weak. And here's the worst part: I think it would get me off even if it ultimately caused harm to the relationship.

So I decided to write. Maybe putting all this down would clear my head.

But then I made a mistake.

I gave her my old laptop. I did delete my story from the laptop, but one day the old laptop broke again. I was in a rush, so I let her borrow my new one.

Life got crazy. Allie got in trouble in school for fighting over an iPad of all things. Events got blurry. It never occurred to me that Dropbox would automatically upload this file to the new machine.

But it did.

A few weeks later, Allie's school crisis behind us, I got the old laptop fixed. Meanwhile, I was back on the new machine. Back to this story, unsure of where it should go next.

Then Beth read it. I'm assuming she read every damning word. I do know that she made it to the end.

She's sleeping behind me, but I don't need her confession.

I might as well end the story here.

No, I'll let her end it. Because she typed it right into the story. Because I know I didn't write this.

And I'm sitting here reading it now, reading what she wrote over and over again, trying to parse the meanings, realizing she must have read this book pretty damn carefully if she knew to put the most important lines in italics, just like I did.

And as I type in the glow of the bedroom desk, while she sleeps soundly only eight feet away from me, I can't think of another way to end the book.

Maybe there's a better way. But these are the cards I have been dealt, and I'm honestly not sure what the next move is. I'm not sure the next move is mine.

Because this is what she wrote:

Be very careful what you wish for.

ALEX HATHAWAY, ALSO THE author of *From Housewife to Cuckoldress: How I Took Sexual Control of a Marriage in Crisis,* is fascinated by the erotic power of sexual taboos and the adventures that can be had by exploring them. An author whose relationships have evolved from vanilla to anything but, Alex has a particular interest in writing about cuckolding and the unconventional sexual fulfillment it can provide.

You can find Alex on the Web at:
alexcuckoldstories.fannypress.com.